JANETTE OKE
&
T. DAVIS BUNN

The Distant Beacon

BETHANY HOUSE PUBLISHERS
MINNEAPOLIS, MINNESOTA 55438

The Distant Beacon
Copyright © 2002
Janette Oke & T. Davis Bunn

Cover illustration and design by Dan Thornberg

Published by Bethany House Publishers
A Ministry of Bethany Fellowship International
11400 Hampshire Avenue South
Bloomington, Minnesota 55438
www.bethanyhouse.com

Printed in the United States of America by
Bethany Press International, Bloomington, Minnesota 55438

ISBN 0-7642-2600-2 (Trade Paper)
ISBN 0-7642-2601-0 (Hardcover)
ISBN 0-7642-2603-7 (Large Print)
ISBN 0-7642-2602-9 (Audio)

Library of Congress Cataloging-in-Publication Data

Oke, Janette, 1935–
    The distant beacon / by Janette Oke & T. Davis Bunn.
        p.   cm. — (Song of Acadia)
    ISBN 0-7642-2601-0
    ISBN 0-7642-2600-2 (pbk.)
    1. United States—History—Revolution, 1775–1783—Fiction.
2. Acadians—Fiction. I. Bunn, T. Davis, 1952- II. Title.
    PR9199.3.O38 D57   2002
    813'.54—dc21   2001005676

JANETTE OKE was born in Champion, Alberta, during the depression years, to a Canadian prairie farmer and his wife. She is a graduate of Mountain View Bible College in Didsbury, Alberta, where she met her husband, Edward. They were married in May of 1957 and went on to pastor churches in Indiana as well as Calgary and Edmonton, Canada.

The Okes have three sons and one daughter and are enjoying the addition of grandchildren to the family. Edward and Janette have both been active in their local church, serving in various capacities as Sunday school teachers and board members. They make their home near Calgary, Alberta.

T. DAVIS BUNN, a native of North Carolina, is a former international business executive whose career has taken him to over forty countries in Europe, Africa, and the Middle East. With topics as diverse as romance, history, and intrigue, Bunn's books continue to reach readers of all ages and interests. He and his wife, Isabella, reside near Oxford, England.

By Janette Oke

Celebrating the Inner Beauty of Woman
Dana's Valley*
Janette Oke's Reflections on the Christmas Story
The Matchmakers
Nana's Gift
The Red Geranium

CANADIAN WEST
When Calls the Heart   When Breaks the Dawn
When Comes the Spring   When Hope Springs New
Beyond the Gathering Storm
When Tomorrow Comes

LOVE COMES SOFTLY
Love Comes Softly   Love's Unending Legacy
Love's Enduring Promise   Love's Unfolding Dream
Love's Long Journey   Love Takes Wing
Love's Abiding Joy   Love Finds a Home

A PRAIRIE LEGACY
The Tender Years   A Quiet Strength
A Searching Heart   Like Gold Refined

SEASONS OF THE HEART
Once Upon a Summer   Winter Is Not Forever
The Winds of Autumn   Spring's Gentle Promise

WOMEN OF THE WEST
The Calling of Emily Evans   A Bride for Donnigan
Julia's Last Hope   Heart of the Wilderness
Roses for Mama   Too Long a Stranger
A Woman Named Damaris   The Bluebird and the Sparrow
They Called Her Mrs. Doc   A Gown of Spanish Lace
The Measure of a Heart   Drums of Change

Janette Oke: A Heart for the Prairie
Biography by Laurel Oke Logan

*with Laurel Oke Logan

"These are the times that try men's souls."

—Thomas Paine, 1776

Prologue

Anne's desk, situated by the lead-paned window in her apartment's front parlor, overlooked the manor house gardens. Normally she liked to sit there only when toddler John was playing on the rug at her feet. Otherwise she preferred to do her letter writing in the library, along with all the paper work related to the villagers. Uncle Charles would join her there, reading the papers sent down from London and playing with John—three generations of family joined by a love so strong Anne often felt overwhelmed by how blessed they truly were.

But this letter was one best written away from any possibility of interruption. Charles liked to read passages to her from the papers, or ask her opinion on various matters about the estate, or point out John's latest feat—whether rolling a ball under the settee where no one could reach it, or saying a new word, or beaming out of his small round face. Anne could not abide such interferences today. She already had put off this letter far too long.

The day was uncommonly warm for an early English spring. Through her open window Anne could hear several robins, their song brief and hesitant, as though they too could scarcely believe the overly wet season might be drawing to a close. That was how she would start her letter, she decided as she dipped the quill into the inkstand.

How it had rained steadily for seven weeks, halting only when the wind rose and the clouds, gray and burly, scuttled across the heavens. Today was the first sunshine she had seen since late February. Drifting in from the window came the smell of damp earth, the faint promise of new beginnings. Yes, a good place to begin her letter to Nicole.

Once she completed that first paragraph, the words began to flow more smoothly. Anne wrote in a conventional manner, as though they were together in the room, rather than separated by a vast ocean. She remarked on how comfortable she had become with her English surroundings, living in her uncle Charles's great manor house, working on projects of education, of faith, in the surrounding communities. How unusual it was that she had grown so rooted here, to the point where the only time she noted it was when she wrote to her North American family and reflected on her *other* home. While she missed them deeply, she found herself to be well satisfied and settled here in Britain.

To see the words *satisfied* and *settled* on the paper, she confessed, seemed strange to her. Anne felt almost frightened to see that idea resting there, glistening in the sunlight, drying into permanence. But she *was* settled. And here was another word she had never expected to use so readily again, she thought as she stared out the window. *Hope.* Hope for a future. One that might bring new happiness, new contentment, even perhaps new children.

There she stopped, but only for a moment. Not because she was reluctant to continue. The letter had been coming swiftly, easily, yet she needed to pause nonetheless. Anne gazed at the distant hills, beyond the little river that ran through the valley on Charles's estate. She heard the lowing of cattle released from their winter quarters; the sound caused a shiver to travel through her slight frame. Her first husband, Cyril, seemed very close just then.

How he would have loved this place and this work. But he was three years in the grave, lost to the grippe back in Nova Scotia soon after hostilities broke out between Britain and the American colonies. Cyril had been a wonderful doctor and a caring husband, and her soul would never again be fully restored. But wounds heal, even this one. Just as a person learned to get on with life after losing a limb, so she too had learned to adjust, to make do. Which was all she had expected for herself. She had her dear sweet little John, she had her family, she had her work with the village women and children. It was far more than anyone could ask for, certainly more than she deserved, she was sure.

Anne's pen raced to catch up with her thoughts as she wrote to her sister and best friend. Another joy that had warmed the winter months. Uncle Charles's health was improving. Ever since he had spoken out publicly in support of the colonials and their battle for independence, Charles had been shunned by society. As a result, they had closed up the London house and spent the entire winter in the country, alone and quiet. Their only visitor had been Cyril's mother, Judith, a widow of many years. Nothing seemed to help Charles in body, mind, and spirit more than Judith's visits, not even baby John. It was a wonder, Anne wrote, to see the love between these two people grow.

And now it was time to speak of what Nicole had perhaps already surmised. She took a deep breath, and her pen scratched and dipped and flowed ever more swiftly. Anne too had wonders and miracles to share. The winter just past had seen her grow increasingly close to Thomas, the young lawyer representing Charles's affairs. They had found a spirit of harmony and purpose; they shared a faith and a vision for lives filled with mission and giving. Three weeks ago, Thomas had asked for her hand in marriage.

After prayer and deep soul searching, she had accepted the next day.

And then just two days later, Anne continued to write, Charles had asked Judith to marry him. The four had talked long about plans and decided they would celebrate a joint wedding—a private, simple affair here in the country.

That same week Anne had written Andrew and Catherine, also to Henri and Louise, with this announcement. The difficult letter was this one. The others lay upon her desk, waiting for her to gather up her resolve and write Nicole. All this Anne explained to her sister. She had been so worried about this letter. And not because she would describe their wedding plans. Those details were minor, especially as they all intended a quiet ceremony with no advance notice given to London society.

Anne forced her hand along the page. She confessed how she couldn't write this news without including her concerns for Nicole.

Anne knew Nicole had never known the feeling of truly belonging—not in Louisiana's Cajun country, where Henri and Louise had eventually made their home, nor in Nova Scotia with her parents by birth. And particularly not here in England where Charles had brought her with the hope of making Nicole his heir. The time Nicole had spent in England was marked by a multitude of disappointed suitors. She had known only one love, and Cajun Jean Dupree had proved to be little more than a rogue. Nicole had never felt bound to either a place or a purpose. Anne's own happiness and sense of belonging served only to heighten this lack, and it was this that laced through the words taking shape on the page.

As hard as this is to put on paper, Anne went on, *I must write and tell you this because I love you so. Despite the differences in our nature, and despite the distance which separates us, I want you to know that I am always your loving sister—more than if we shared the same parents. And in one sense we do—both sets!*

The sun chose that moment to slip around the corner of the house and fall with uncommon brilliance on the page. Anne paused for more ink. She recalled as she had a thousand times before the bittersweet memory of those two young mothers of long ago and the agonizing circumstances that had left them to love and raise the other's infant as their own.

It will take months for this letter to arrive, she finally continued on the glowing page, *and months more for your answer to come back. I will pray in the meantime for God's continued blessing and guidance in your life and give to you what I have found for myself. Each and every day will I pray for you, dearest sister. I close with this prayer upon my lips and my heart, and send to you my love, Anne.*

Chapter 1

Catherine stood by her kitchen window, the place which had become the center of her existence. Never before had she felt closed in by her life, or considered her world too small. But this winter had been the loneliest she had ever known, with her father's health failing and the storms as bad as any she could remember and Andrew often away. To make matters worse, there had been only one letter from Anne and this one back in November. And none at all from Nicole. Catherine's isolation grew with each day that she did not hear from her beloved daughters.

She was certain they both had written. She knew this in her bones, that they thought of her and prayed for her and wrote regularly. It wasn't their fault, in spite of the fact that they each were too far away. It was the war.

The window was open now, in spite of the chill wind still shaking a fist at spring. Her father, John Price, dozed by the fire, the quilt pulled tight against his chin. He seldom moved very far these days, and he ate next to nothing. They didn't speak of his condition much, though everyone in the village knew the old man was merely biding his time, waiting for the silent knock on his door. He had made his peace, was about all John would say if asked how he was faring. Occasionally he would add that he was growing impatient to bow in person before his Lord. Whenever he spoke like this, Catherine was forced to quell the immediate pang in her heart, sometimes fleeing to her bedroom to compose herself again.

The breakfast dishes done, the lane in front of their house empty, and it would be another hour or so before she would start preparing the midday meal. Yet she remained standing there, watching the sunlight cast upon the brown earth. Patches of half-melted snow were all that was left of the longest winter she had ever endured. A single bird chirped once, the crystal sound echoing the longing in her heart for Anne, for Nicole.

As though sensing her sorrow, Andrew opened the bedroom door and moved toward her, his slippers treading light across the bare wood planks. The one good thing about the entire winter, the one blessing she recounted each time she bowed her head in prayer, was that Andrew was as strong as he had been in years. The endowment from Charles had meant he could give up his leather-working trade that so drained his energy, as well as buy himself a fine horse. For Andrew wasn't only providing pastoral care for a growing community, he was also constantly visiting those soldiers camped nearby. So many needs, and so many of them truly dire. The horse had provided transport and saved him precious time.

Andrew gripped Catherine's arms from behind and leaned in close enough to breathe gently against her hair. He did this often, especially before another journey, holding her so tight she finally had to pull away and take a long, slow breath.

Despite the worry and the quiet mournfulness of another day without any news, Catherine couldn't help but smile as Andrew buried his face in her hair. She asked her husband, "What do you smell?"

"Flour," he murmured, not retreating.

"That would be the biscuits from breakfast."

"And soap."

"Though it has been three days since I last washed those tresses so close to your nose."

"And love."

The quip she might have said caught in her throat. Catherine let herself be guided around by his strong hands until she stared directly into his eyes. "I do love you, my husband."

"And I you." His face still held the chiseled quality of the lieutenant and warrior she had married twenty-three years ago. But now his features were overlaid by creases of age and concern and also the gentle fervor of one who lived to serve his Lord. From his eyes shone the clearest light, a sign just for her that intimated she was indeed loved.

Andrew told her, "I heard in town of another encampment along the Halifax road. I think I will ride out and make sure all is well."

"You said yesterday you wouldn't leave until after our noon meal—."

"There are storm clouds gathering out back. I saw them through the bedroom window. I should go while the day is dry."

"I'll pack you provisions for the journey." But Andrew continued to hold her close and watch her with luminous gaze. "What is it?" she asked.

"I was praying earlier."

Catherine nodded. This she knew. It was another of the many gifts that had come to them with the acceptance of Charles's funds. Andrew now had time for study and prayer every morning, something she was certain had done much to improve his health.

"And I had the strongest impression," Andrew continued. "Not words, mind you. But almost that powerful, and certainly as clear."

"The Lord spoke to you?"

"So it seemed to me then. And now." A hand rose to gently stroke her cheek. "I believe our daughters are well. They are fine."

Catherine nodded in agreement, for it was this reassurance that had made it possible for her to continue to live each day as normally as she did.

"And I think," said Andrew, looking straight into her eyes, "that we shall be hearing from them very soon."

Catherine felt her distress rise. "But how? You hear the war news and the rumors more than I. Nothing is getting through the blockades. Nothing!"

It was no longer possible to ignore the war. The conflict had become woven into the fabric of their daily lives. The actual battles remained well to the south and west of them, yet war now touched every aspect of their world.

The Halifax harbor was jammed with ships, either joining the New York and Boston blockades or ferrying troops to the conflict in Quebec. Even when the roads had become impassable from vicious winds and lashing snow, still the news had managed to filter through, carried by desperate refugees. And almost all the news was of death and darkness.

Andrew did not shush her so much as soothe away her words as he caressed her cheek. "I cannot tell you how I feel these things, or why. But that is how it seems to me. That we shall soon be hearing from them both, and the news will be good. Very good indeed."

Catherine slipped out of her husband's grasp and turned to the worktable. She didn't want to send Andrew off with tears. "Let me see to your meal," she said briskly, managing to wipe her eyes while pretending to adjust her apron. "I believe there is some of that good salt beef left along with biscuits from breakfast . . . and the last of the dried apples."

Nicole resisted the urge to crane out the carriage window yet again. There was nothing to be seen save more trees and another stretch of empty road. "Why is it taking so long?" she asked again, recognizing it was a childish query.

She knew Gordon Goodwind would not respond. She spoke because she could no longer hold on to her impatience.

After a sharp lurch the carriage jarred to a halt. The horses in front whinnied a protest as they jangled their leads. The conveyance rested at an uncomfortable angle. Nicole watched Gordon lean out his window as the driver leaped down from his station. She knew the tidings before Gordon moved back in and the driver clambered up on the step to report, "Looks like we're good and stuck this time, missus."

"What, again?"

"They's been dragging cannon through here, from the looks of things." The driver was an impossibly cheerful soul, someone Nicole would have loved to visit with under different circumstances. "Either that or plowing furrows down the lane. We'll have to unharness the horses and drag her out backwards, that's my guess."

"We might as well get out and have something to eat," Gordon offered.

Nicole bit down hard on her tongue. There was nothing to be gained from expressing again her impatience. The men were doing the best job they could. That they had come this far at all was a miracle. More than that, a series of miracles had occurred, one after another, as though angels assisted and protected her at every step.

Even so, the voyage from England had taken nearly five months. Had she known she would be forced to fight her way across the tides of conflict, Nicole doubted she would have had the fortitude to begin the journey at all.

Twice their ship had been waylaid by the British. The first time was on the high seas. A war squadron suddenly appeared out of a squall line and sent three shots through their rigging before the captain could convince the hostile ships that he was in fact their ally. Apparently the French had taken to flying false colors as a means of getting their ships through to help the Americans. Which had done little to ease their captain's anger at being struck by one of the king's own. Only his wife, who served as Nicole's official chaperone and companion on the voyage, managed to hold off a dangerous confrontation.

A month later, following the frigid winter crossing of the North Atlantic, they had been stopped by the British blockade off New York. These blockade ships held royal grants, which permitted the requisition of all foodstuffs and armaments from vessels sailing through the blockade line. Their own stores already had been reduced to primarily hardtack and jerky. To their captain's dismay, the blockade lieutenant had scrounged their last wheel of Wesleyan cheese and the remaining half barrel of apples, not to mention the better part of their gunpowder and shot.

New York proved to be firmly in British hands. The city was crammed tight with troops and Loyalists who were fleeing the conflict in other areas. The place held to such a chaotic din that Nicole made no protest when Gordon, who was serving as her escort and protector, suggested they stay berthed on the ship. So there they had remained for three of the most tense and frustrating weeks of Nicole's life. The wind had blown continuously from the north, causing every rope and every stanchion to grow icicles as long as her arm.

Prices within the city itself were beyond belief, for the Revolutionaries had cut off all the roads leading north so that only a trickle of supplies was coming in from the Loyalist colonies farther south. One morning Nicole witnessed a refugee family buying a sack of cornmeal in exchange for a solid silver candelabra.

The garrison commander had wanted to requisition both the ship and all the men. Only two factors saved them. One was Gordon's offer to travel north for supplies and more troops. The second was a surprise her uncle Charles had kept well hidden, one she had discovered when they were more than halfway through their journey. At the bottom of one of her trunks, amidst a mass of other papers related to her new landholdings in western Massachusetts, Nicole found a charter officially naming her the Viscountess Harrow. Charles had attached a terse note, stating simply that the sanctioned title might come in handy in these uncertain times. Indeed it had. Not even the commander of the New York garrison was willing to risk royal ire by depriving a viscountess of her ship. As had been planned, Captain Madden and his wife remained in New York. At Captain Madden's suggestion, Nicole had formally contracted the vessel and its crew to take her north, with Captain Gordon Goodwind as her official escort. A family, desperate to flee the war, begged for passage north, as they had kin homesteading on the outskirts of Halifax. Nicole was happy to acquiesce since the woman and her two daughters would provide female companionship for the remaining journey.

The voyage to Nova Scotia had taken another month. Twice they had spotted sails on the horizon and elected to detour far out to sea rather than risk running afoul of a French man-o'-war.

Halifax itself turned out to be in colossal chaos. They had berthed next to a hulk so blasted and war blackened that Nicole couldn't even read her name. The city was one mass of troops and Loyalists. The roads were nearly impassable, more closely resembling half-frozen swamps than lanes. Horses strained and fought to drag even empty carts through the mire. Men and animals alike were spattered in red mud up to their chests. Planks had been laid across the busiest thoroughfares, but one wrong step and one was plunged into muck. Most women elected to be carried from one covered walkway to another—that or stay at home. For it wasn't merely the mud and the endless wet that made the streets of Halifax unsafe that long winter.

Once again Nicole's title had proved to be a boon. Rooms were made available in the governor's own manor, and Nicole had enjoyed her first full bath and fresh hot meal in weeks. Three days they had stayed there, enduring a barrage of war news and ugly rumors. Time and again Gordon was urged to take up the king's arms and join the struggle. He had carefully countered that his immediate allegiance was already given to those who had entrusted him with the vessel at his charge. At such times Nicole felt her feelings surge to the bursting point for the young officer. Without him she knew she would have made no progress whatsoever.

When they had found it impossible to beg or buy transport, the governor offered Nicole his personal carriage. Normally she would have balked at the idea of arriving home in such grand style. But after all the frustration and delays, she nearly wept with gratitude. But here again their way had been met by further frustration, more obstacles. First there had been no horses trained to pull in tandem. Then the rain had set in once more, which made the roads worse still.

Finally there came three sunny days in a row, enough for the driver to pronounce the roads fit for travel. Only then it seemed as if the entire city had elected to start off along the Georgetown road. Nicole had never seen such congestion of beast and vehicles. What should have been a long day's journey, two at the most, had stretched into four days, then five and still there was no sight of George-town, no sign they were even drawing near to her beloved parents.

As the driver's young assistant handed down the hamper to Gordon with their daily provisions, Nicole stretched her legs while keeping an eye on the road ahead. By now her habits were well-known to all. At every halt she would be the first to survey the scene before them, searching her memory for any sign of familiarity. So much had changed. The narrow trail had been broadened and cut with trenches from the many heavy carts. In earlier days it was rare that they would pass other travelers more than once between the rising of the sun and its descent. If they happened upon someone in the late afternoon, it was tradition to stop and see if these were folk with whom they might camp overnight. Bandits preyed upon travelers, and there was greater safety in numbers.

Finding company was no longer a concern. Even this far from Halifax the road was still clogged with traffic. Much of the valley, Nicole noticed, had been cleared. The forests were razed back, and newly built cabins now spouted smoke.

Here on the road a handcart was tucked up tight beneath the boughs of a nearby tree, with an exhausted family sprawled alongside. Nicole's heart twisted at the sight of two bedraggled young girls, their tattered boots held together with twine. Nothing but their eyes moved as she walked toward them.

She gave them all a smile and then, as was the custom, addressed the man. "Good day to you, sir."

But it was the wife who responded first. "It's a fine day for traveling, missus. At long last."

"Aye, for them as can travel in fitting style," the husband muttered, casting a dark glance at Nicole's steeds and carriage.

"Enough, Harry," scolded the woman. She turned to Nicole. "Don't mind him, m'lady. We've been sorely put upon by them what's selling goods back in Halifax."

"Which she well knows and profits from, by all accounts," the husband spat out.

"Harry, I'm warning you now." The woman's smile was bent sharply by her weariness. "We came in with plans to provision up in the capital, but the prices—"

"I understand." Because she hadn't been invited to sit, Nicole remained standing. "The prices they are charging are beyond belief."

"If it's so for folks in ribbons and lace, imagine what it's been for the likes of us." The husband's bile could not be held down. He waved an angry hand toward his wagon, piled high with their possessions. "I paid more for that pushcart than should have cost me for a proper rig and mules!"

Before the woman could direct another reproach toward her husband, Nicole said, "You have every reason to be upset." She gestured back to where Gordon and the boy were unpacking the hamper. "We have extra provisions we are happy to share."

The woman's eyes gleamed at the words, and the two young girls scrambled to their feet. But the man growled, "We don't take charity from nobody. I've worked hard all my life, I have, and earned my way fair and square."

Nicole knelt in the dirt beside their cart. She had worn the same traveling garments every day of the journey. They had met such people at every stop, and she didn't want fine clothing to form yet another barrier. The carriage itself appeared so filthy and pitted by hard use that the royal crest was now a single colorless gray. Yet the social distance between her and this family was far too great, which meant she had no choice but confess, "I too have paid my dues upon the road, sir."

The man's mouth twisted hard. "You?"

"I know it would be easy to disbelieve me. But it is true. My family lost everything when I was younger than your own sweet girls, in another war. And we were forced to journey against our will." She indicated Gordon where he stood waiting. "Please permit me to offer you what I can only wish had been granted to us."

The woman replied hastily, "We thank you, missus." To her husband she insisted, "For the children, Harry."

When the husband remained intent upon the ground by his feet, Nicole stood and smiled for the girls alone. "Would you like to see inside the carriage?"

Their eyes grew round. The younger of the two inserted a finger into her mouth, but the older one piped up, "Yes, missus. We would."

"Come along then." She took one by each hand and walked them over to where the driver was unhitching the steeds. "What is your name, my friend?"

"Maggie, and my sister here is Nel." She pointed at the lead stallion. "Can I touch him?"

Nicole led the girl to where she could stroke the horse's nose. "Isn't he a grand big horse, now?"

"We had three such, but none as nice as him. What's his name?"

"I don't know. This isn't my carriage, you see."

"Whose is it, then?"

"A man who wanted to help me return home."

"Where's home for you, missus?"

Nicole lowered the girl back to earth. "Georgetown."

The young girl brightened. "That's where we're headed, missus. Papa's bought us a parcel up by George-town. I remember him saying the name."

"That's wonderful. You'll like it there. Georgetown is

a lovely place." She walked over and opened the carriage door. "Come have a look."

The two girls scrambled inside. They exclaimed over the plush seats and the dusty red curtains that could be pulled down over the windows, and how they looked out at the world from up high. When they had climbed back down, the elder sister said, "We had us a farm once."

"Where?"

"Yorktown. But we lost it. My dad says it's on account of us backing the wrong horse. But I don't know what he meant. We only had the three and two mules, and we sold them when we had to leave."

Gordon walked over and handed her a sack of goods, by now well used to Nicole's kindness to strangers. She had resisted the urge to tell him much of her early days, about her immediate connections to all these who had been uprooted from their homes in that ceaseless search for security, for peace. She felt it would only have forged bonds that were already threatening her heart with uncertainties. But Gordon seemed to sense her need to give from what she had, and she admired him all the more for not requiring a defense of her generosity.

Gordon rejoined the driver and his assistant, and together they began rocking the carriage out of the ditch. The older girl watched them for a moment, then asked, "Please, missus, will there be the guns in the night?"

"I'm sorry—?"

"Up Georgetown way. Where we're headed." The girl brushed tangled tresses away from her eyes, leaving a dirty streak across her forehead. "Will there be the guns again? They scared little Nel something awful, them guns."

The little girl whimpered around the finger she had kept in her mouth. Her sister draped a protective arm about the little one's shoulders. She continued in her piping voice, "That's why we had to leave in the end. We didn't want to go. But them guns, they kept coming closer. Every night they went booming and flashing, till one night they was right in the next valley over."

Nicole resisted the urge to sweep up both girls in a fierce embrace. The parents were watching closely and might not care to see a stranger hold their children so. "I am absolutely certain," she said, forcing her voice to hold steady, "there will be no guns around Georgetown, not in the day or the night."

"It's all right, then." Maggie hugged little Nel to herself. "See there, what did Papa tell you? We'll be safe and sound—you just wait."

Nicole walked the two girls back over to their parents and set the sack of provisions at their mother's feet. "My father is vicar of Georgetown."

"Your father?" The husband seemed to have difficulty fitting his mind around that news.

"That's right. He and my mother do all they can to help out newcomers like yourself. I urge you to seek them out."

He slowly rose to his feet, slipping the sweat-stained hat from his head. "Your pardon, missus. I thought, well, with the carriage and all—"

"It's not mine. I've been away for almost two years, and this was lent to me to help speed my way home." She gestured to the sack. "Please accept this as a token of welcome to your new home."

Gordon called, "Nicole!" When she turned, he said, "The carriage is free now. We can eat and continue on our way."

"One moment." She turned back and urged the parents, "Please contact Pastor Andrew Harrow as soon as you can. And do not consider what they offer as charity. They seek only to build a better, closer community. When you can, give to the next ones who arrive and are in need."

To free them from any necessity to find words of

thanks, Nicole bent down and placed both hands on the shoulders of young Maggie. "Remember what I say to you, little friend. Hold fast to God, and be strong. This too shall pass."

She then strode back to the carriage, heartsore at the matter-of-fact way the child had learned to carry her suffering.

She looked at Gordon as he watched her approach. They had seen this kind of hardship numerous times before. They moved to the side of the road and bowed their heads to thank the Divine Creator and Sustainer of Life for the gifts before them, simple as they might be.

Chapter 2

Finally the road rounded a bend that seemed carved from Nicole's most heartfelt memory. She could no longer contain herself and cried for the carriage to halt. Before the driver had fully reined in the horses, Nicole opened the carriage door and dropped to the ground, almost spilling head over heels. But she managed to keep her balance as she hurried forward. A hundred yards along the trail, a hundred fifty, then she suddenly stopped. She pressed hands tightly to her heaving chest.

Up ahead, rising from the browns and grays of an early spring landscape, rose the slender spire of her father's church. It seemed only fitting that this be the first signal of her return.

Nicole flew back to the carriage. "Hand down that small trunk! Please. No, not that one, the other bound in leather."

Gordon was standing at the door of the carriage, watching her curiously. "What is it?"

She accepted the trunk from the driver, set it on the ground, and found her hands to be trembling so much she made hard going of the straps.

"Nicole, what's the matter?" Gordon asked again.

She finally got the trunk unlatched and flipped open the lid. On top, wrapped in clean bunting, was the dress she had decided upon while still on board the vessel. A white frock, the simplest she owned, the only decoration was tiny mother-of-pearl buttons and a froth of lace rising from waist to neck and adorning each wrist.

"Nicole, my dear, Georgetown is but an hour's ride ahead of us."

"Yes, that is so. You don't think I can meet my parents wearing four days of road dust, do you?" She dug through the trunk to find a pair of shoes of ivory kid leather. She glanced at Gordon. "Do you have anything finer to wear than that dusty old greatcoat?"

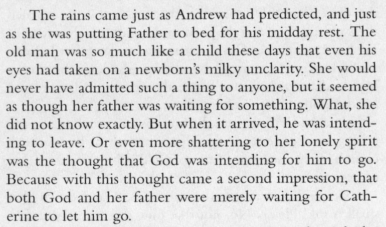

The rains came just as Andrew had predicted, and just as she was putting Father to bed for his midday rest. The old man was so much like a child these days that even his eyes had taken on a newborn's milky unclarity. She would never have admitted such a thing to anyone, but it seemed as though her father was waiting for something. What, she did not know exactly. But when it arrived, he was intending to leave. Or even more shattering to her lonely spirit was the thought that God was intending for him to go. Because with this thought came a second impression, that both God and her father were merely waiting for Catherine to let him go.

She sat by his bed as she had many times through the difficult winter, when ice and snow had closed the roads and she couldn't make the journey to her beloved French settlement a day's ride northeast of Georgetown. She would sit here by her slumbering father and listen to the snow and wind and think about her earlier days with a clarity that words could never provide.

She would recall her beloved friend Louise and their meeting place high above their two villages—and the day

they exchanged babies, the journey to Halifax for the doctor to see to her little one. Then came the horrible day of
Acadian expulsion. Those nearly two decades of not
knowing what had happened to her baby, to Louise and
Henri. The years of loving and raising little Anne as their
own. Here there was no pain to the memories, not even
over the loss of her own Nicole. She thought of her by
that name now, which was as it should be. And she prayed
for them all.

By the time she emerged from Father John's room, the
rain had ceased its thunderous drumming on the roof. A
few moments later, while she was washing the midday
dishes, the sun reappeared. The air beyond her kitchen
window sparkled with a special clarity now, every scent
etched against the backdrop of wet earth and a clean
spring breeze. The church bell rang the hour, and all the
world seemed to shimmer in cadence with the chime.
Even a gentle birdsong held a strength echoed by the
whinny of a horse determinedly shaking its bridle.

A driver's whip cracked through the clear afternoon
Catherine paused in her chores and squinted out the window. Beyond her range of vision, an angry driver used his
whip a second time and shouted, "Ho there, you! Pull
your weight now, giddap!"

The horse neighed in protest. No, not just one horse.
Obviously several of them were straining hard against a
heavy load and the mud from this most recent rain. Catherine stood there amazed that any driver in his right mind
would attempt to force his steeds through the aftermath of
a spring downpour.

Then, to her astonishment, four horses rounded the
corner, heaving and straining to pull a stately carriage.
Catherine raised a hand and rubbed her eyes. The picture
seemed drawn from a childhood fairy tale, yet there it was.
A royal crest adorned the travel-stained door.

She watched as a young man leaned out the window

and called, "All right, that's far enough."

"And high time too," the driver shouted back. Even in his mud-spattered state, the man was dressed in regal finery. And the horses. Though with muck dripping from their chests and each one foam draped and blowing hard, she knew these were magnificent animals. The driver slackened the reins and threw on the hand brake. "Whoa there, ease up now."

It seemed to Catherine that half the village followed in the lane behind the carriage. And all of the children. Well they should, for it was only the fact that she could see them chattering and pointing that allowed her to believe her own eyes.

The driver climbed down from his high perch, when the carriage door opened and the young man said, "No, no, Samuel, you go ahead and see to your horses."

As the driver moved away toward the horses, Catherine saw he was dressed in the formal blue of a naval officer, with long hair tied back in a blue velvet ribbon. He inspected the muddy lane by the carriage, then reached inside and pulled out a greatcoat, rather the worse for wear. He stepped down, ignoring his polished boots now in muck beyond his ankles. Then he did the most gallant thing Catherine had ever seen. He spread his coat to make a clean path from the carriage to their stone front walkway.

He turned and reached up a hand, and Catherine's hands went to her mouth at the sight emerging from the carriage. Too young for a queen, a duchess, perhaps. The young lady's white dress seemed to float about her. An awestruck murmur rose from the villagers gathered around as she stepped carefully to the ground and trod across the greatcoat.

She arrived at the gate and fumbled with the latch as one blind. She was crying. Raising her head to search the housefront, she called, "Mama?"

"Nicole!" Catherine flew around the kitchen table,

spilling a bowl of vegetables in her haste. She fumbled with her own front-door latch until, with a second cry, she hammered it back with the palm of her hand. Nicole was still standing by the front gate, unable to make it open. Catherine ran down the path and reached over the gate to sweep her daughter up in an embrace so fierce nothing could hold them apart. Not the gate, nor time, nor linen finery, nor life's changes, nor the cheering of all those crowded along the lane. Nothing.

Chapter 3

"I didn't want the carriage to come down the lane at all," Nicole said again. She sat, her back straight, with Catherine's best teacup and saucer placed carefully on her knee. "But the mud was so very bad, and Gordon insisted."

"It's fine, dear. I couldn't care less about such matters." Catherine noticed for the first time in years that the handle of Nicole's cup was chipped, and the cup didn't match the saucer. Even worse, Gordon's cup was cracked from rim to base.

"She halted us an hour's ride outside the village to change into this fine white frock you see," Gordon noted with a small smile. He stood by the unlit fireplace, almost as one ready to snap to attention. Not even his stockinged feet could diminish the young man's military bearing. "I couldn't permit her to muddy up those shoes walking across your village lane." He hastily added, "Not that I mean to denigrate your town, madame. Georgetown is as fine a hamlet as I have seen. It puts most English towns to shame, and I mean that most sincerely."

"Thank you." Catherine gripped her cup without raising it to her lips. She wanted to reach out and again draw her daughter close but found herself gazing in awe at this refined young woman.

Nicole's poise wasn't just in her bearing. She spoke with the finest diction, her French accent a mere trace now. Her face was dusted with some powder, and she carried about herself the fragrance of Oriental spices. Her hair was bound up in a fashion Catherine could not even begin to fathom.

Nicole reached out and took hold of Catherine's hand. Even here there was discomfort, when she only wanted to recapture the first moments of joy at their reunion. Catherine looked down at the two hands and wished she could hide away her own, red and winter-chapped as they were.

"I'm so glad to see you, Mama. I have waited so long, I can hardly believe it is true. How have you been?"

Catherine willed herself to give back a taste of the love and care she found in her daughter's eyes. At least this had not changed. And yet it had, for the person who gazed at her was a woman indeed, and the expression had deepened and strengthened such that even here Catherine found herself stumbling over the confession, "Missing you—."

"And I you," Nicole said. A sheen of tears appeared. But the woman who was her daughter showed her strength of will. She lifted her chin and blinked repeatedly, holding back the flow. Catherine wanted to squeeze the hand she held and tell her daughter to let go, to release the tears and weep for them both. But she couldn't bring herself to speak, and Nicole smiled tremulously at the young officer and said, "Look at me. I'm such a ninny."

"Not anything like that," Gordon reassured her. The young man straightened to full attention as the rear door opened.

"I heard voices," Father John said, unsteadily making his way through the doorway, adjusting his suspenders.

"Grandfather!" Nicole hurried to embrace the old man.

"Good gracious, child. Could this be you?" The old

man's eyes sharpened as they hadn't in months. He smiled and said, "You leave a fine young lass and come back to me a duchess."

"That is exactly what I thought," Catherine said, not able to keep the pride from her voice. "A duchess has come to visit us."

"My dear sweet Nicole," Father John said. "You do us all proud."

Nicole led the old man over to the fireplace. "Grandfather, may I present Gordon Goodwind, who has escorted me all the way from England."

Gordon gave the military half bow. "An honor, sir. Nicole has often spoken of you, and always in the highest possible terms."

Catherine watched as the old man's gaze sharpened further still. "An officer, are you?"

"Indeed, sir."

"Navy?"

"Actually, sir, I am with the merchant marine."

"As honorable a position as any." John pointed to the rocker by the fireplace. "Give me a hand with settling my bones, will you?"

"Of course, sir." With Gordon on one side and Catherine on the other, the old man lowered himself into the padded seat.

"Gordon is captain of his own vessel, Grandfather."

"Then obviously there are others who think highly of you, besides my granddaughter." Father John pointed to empty chairs. "Sit yourselves down, the both of you."

Father John inspected them and said, "If I didn't know better, I would say I was looking at royalty."

Gordon cleared his throat. "Actually, sir—"

"Gordon, no," Nicole protested quietly.

"They need to know," Gordon replied. "They are your family."

Nicole dropped her eyes to the hands in her lap.

"Your daughter . . ." Gordon hesitated a moment and glanced at Nicole, clearly hoping for some sign of approval. But she didn't raise her head. "That is, Nicole . . ."

"Out with it, man," Father John said. "We already know her name."

"Yes, sir. That is, well, she is actually a titled lady now."

Catherine couldn't help but stare. "What do you mean?"

"It's nothing, Mama," Nicole said, her face embarrassed. "Really."

"I'm sorry, Miss Nicole, but I must respectfully disagree." Gordon continued in a rush, "Charles has elected to make Anne's son, his closest heir by blood, the lord of the Harrow estate. But he has granted Nicole the title of viscountess."

Catherine knew her mouth was open and she was staring round-eyed at this beloved stranger who was her daughter, yet she could think of nothing to say or do.

Father John, on the other hand, chuckled with glee. The sound was enough to lift even Nicole's uncomfortable gaze. "Is this youth speaking the truth?" he asked.

"I—I believe so, Grandfather."

He laughed even louder. "If that doesn't beat all. The little one who leaves and is lost to us for nigh on twenty years, who then comes back, meets her uncle, and then goes off again, now returns a titled lady!" He slapped his knee. "I've lived to see it all, I have. I can die a happy man."

"Don't say that!" When she realized her daughter had exclaimed the exact same words as well, Catherine covered her mouth. The two of them stared at each other, on the verge of laughter and tears both.

But before they could give vent to either, the front door slammed open against the side wall. Still in his muddy riding boots, Andrew leaped across the room and gathered up his daughter in a tight embrace. He held her there for a long moment, the only sound in the room that of Father John's chuckles.

"Look out there, will you," the old man said, pointing a shaky finger out the door toward the carriage mired almost to its axles before their cottage. The driver and his helper had pulled the horses over to the nearby stable for currying and a good feed. "Almost like the king himself has come for tea."

But Andrew seemed unaware of anything but the fact that he was holding his daughter. "Welcome home, my dear. Welcome home," he whispered.

Catherine felt the bands around her chest begin to ease. Leave it to her husband to see beyond the finery and receive this lovely young woman back as their very own.

Father John smiled up at the pair of them and said, "Careful now, that's a true viscountess you're holding. One of them royals, she is."

Andrew released her enough to stare into the tear-streaked face with a trembling smile. He brushed burnished locks from her damp cheek. "Oh," he said, "I've always known that. Always."

Chapter 4

Many more surprises followed Nicole's arrival. On the second day, Father John had felt well enough to take his first walk through the village since the previous summer. He made his way up their lane toward the village square, Nicole to his right, holding his arm and elbow with both hands, and Gordon doing the same on his left. The two young people so towered over the bent old man that they could exchange glances and remarks over his bowed head. Catherine knew this because she watched them through her kitchen window. She saw how the two of them looked at each other, their glances lingering, and she saw the tenderness come to the young man's stalwart features. Her little window had shown her so much of the world. It now revealed to her two new things. First, that her daughter was deeply in love yet unable to acknowledge it even to herself. And second, that when the young man departed, so too would Nicole.

The third day's noon meal was interrupted by a great clattering of horses and men pulling up outside their cottage. A voice Catherine recognized as one of the village boys piped loud and clear, "This here's the cottage, your lordship, sir! Right through there."

"That's a good lad. Here now, a bright new king's shilling for your trouble."

Gordon was already up and moving for the door. His previous courteous and affable demeanor was gone. In its place was a man who had learned through hardship and trial to bear the mantle of command. He paused only long enough to give his military bow and say to Catherine, "Your pardon, ma'am." He then flung open the door and cried, "I say there, what's the meaning of this?"

"Captain Goodwind?"

"The same."

"I seek the Viscountess Lady Harrow."

"To what purpose, my man?"

"I am purser to his lordship, the governor of Halifax."

"Of course, I recognize you now." Gordon turned back to the little group inside. "Your pardon, Miss Nicole. But I fear this requires your personal attention."

Nicole rose. "Excuse me, Mama."

"Of course, dear." Catherine could scarcely say the term of endearment, for before her stood a lady of regal bearing. Clearly Andrew felt the same. He reached for Catherine's hand as Nicole crossed the front room.

"Good day to you, sir," they heard Nicole say.

"Your pardon, Viscountess, but his lordship urgently requires the carriage, as his other has been damaged by a mud slide. He asks if you might be making the return journey this day."

"That is quite impossible."

Sunlight through the open front door made the room's shadows even deeper. Andrew's face fell into a deep frown of concern. Catherine knew her own features mirrored his reaction. There was no pleasure to be found even in the news that Nicole was remaining with them at least a while longer. Her imminent departure had been all but announced.

The governor's steward said, "Then I must respectfully ask if your ladyship is willing to return by horseback."

"Of course."

"The governor will be most relieved to hear this, ma'am. He apologizes most profusely, but the carriage is to return with us, and without delay. I've brought saddle horses for you and Captain Goodwind. And the packhorse you see here."

"That will do us perfectly well, thank you."

Catherine found the strength to call over, "Nicole dear."

Nicole looked around, instantly transformed to the softer self, the familiar daughter. "Yes, Mama?"

"Ask the gentleman if he has had lunch."

Nicole seemed momentarily at a loss.

Andrew spoke up. "We do not stand upon class in this house, my dear. You should ask the gentleman if he would like to come inside."

"It's not that, Papa," Nicole replied.

It was Gordon who responded, "I fear there is more than just the one gentleman, sir."

Gordon pushed open the door fully. Catherine craned about the table and held her breath at the sight of an entire retinue lined up outside the cottage. A dozen men and more, all bearing the sabers and redcoats of the mighty hussars, were seated upon their elegant steeds.

Turning back to the men, Gordon said, "The lady of the house wishes to inquire if you and your men have brought sufficient provisions."

Although the lead man likely couldn't pierce the interior shadows, he leaned over the horse's head and saluted the house. "My thanks, lady. We have vittles aplenty. But the horses could use some fresh water."

"I'll walk you to the stables." Gordon bowed a second time to Catherine. "Your pardon, ma'am, but I must interrupt this wonderful repast and see to the matter at hand."

"I'll place a cloth over your plate until you return," Catherine answered weakly.

The governor's steward continued, "Your lieutenant has sent the provisional bills of lading for your inspection, Captain. If you don't mind, sir, I request that you review them and formulate your response without delay. We're due back forthwith."

The men and the noise moved down the lane. Catherine felt the sharp pain of departure twist slightly in her heart at the words *bills of lading*. They held the tone of sea journeys and danger and the conflict beyond their sheltered haven. All those things she would keep at arm's length for those she loved.

Catherine watched her daughter return to the table and saw how her features showed no hint of what had just transpired. In fact, they revealed little save a determined calm. But Catherine could see Andrew also watching their daughter, obviously sensing the same things as Catherine. Their daughter was here with them for only a brief time.

Father John seemed utterly untouched by the coming separation. Instead he grinned as he dipped his biscuit into the gravy. "Hussars and the governor's own man, redcoats saluting and horses stamping. All just outside our front gate. That'll set a hawk amidst the village pigeons, you mark my words." His cackle sounded a bit like one of those hawks.

The fourth day of Nicole's visit was the Sabbath. Father John's words proved prophetic, for never had the church been so full. Not on Christmas, nor Easter. People lined the way from the square to where the church stood within its white-fenced green. Father John strode like a man who overnight had shed twenty of his years. Nicole held to his arm and returned the villagers' greetings with quiet warmth. Gordon Goodwind escorted Catherine with a gentleman-officer's serious bearing. He attracted almost as much attention as Nicole. Many Loyalist settlers had migrated north since the American conflict erupted. Most had never exchanged personal greetings with a real British officer before that day. The fact that Gordon Goodwind was a noncombatant and wore the swordless dress uniform of the merchant service mattered not a whit. Bevies of round-eyed boys threw pretend salutes as he passed, and young village girls blushed and giggled behind their hands at the handsome officer.

If only Catherine could give herself fully to the wonder of this good day.

After the service, Nicole joined her mother in preparing the Sabbath meal. Father John dozed quietly by the fire. The day was warm enough for Andrew to invite Gordon to join him on the bench outside their front door. The men's words floated clear and easy through the kitchen window.

"My compliments to you, sir," Gordon said. "Seldom am I moved by church services. But your words and your manner touched me most deeply."

"I am more interested in your normal response," Andrew said in a calm tone, "than by what you felt this day."

"An officer is a man who stands alone. We are trained to rely on our own judgment and the strength of our good right hand."

"I would feel far more comforted to know that God formed a part of this strength."

What Gordon thought of his words being so evidently overheard, Catherine could not tell. But she noticed that Nicole paused in her work to listen as her escort responded, "I am well aware of the Lord, sir."

"You will permit me to speak freely?"

"Of course."

"I wonder if you might be treating our heavenly

Father as you would a distant ally. Someone best kept at arm's length."

"On the contrary, sir. I am certain He is out there and available should I ever have need of Him."

"Alas," Andrew countered. "That is the only time such a conversation might take place between you and your Maker. When one is *required*?"

Gordon's laugh sounded nervous. "I can only hope such a time should never come, sir."

"Of course not," Andrew murmured.

Nicole stood staring at nothing but the blinding sunlight streaming through the window. After a long moment, she sighed quietly and returned to her work.

Following their meal, Nicole asked Andrew, "May I have your permission to walk with Gordon out to the point?"

"Yes, my dear," he said without pause.

When Nicole reached for the wrap she had worn to market the previous day, with its lace trimmings and the lovely butterflies sewn in blue silk, Catherine hastened to offer her own shawl. "For warmth," she murmured.

"Oh yes, thank you."

Catherine handed her daughter the best she owned, a cotton and linen mix she had woven herself. Looking at the rough weave wrapped about Nicole and her auburn tresses spilling over her shoulders, Catherine found her heart moved by this remarkable blend of the daughter she had sent off and the one who had returned to her. On impulse she reached for Nicole and held her close and then somehow managed to whisper, "You are my sweet, dear daughter."

"Oh, Mama."

But when Catherine had seen the couple off and returned to where the two men sat by the fire, she found her husband staring at the glowing embers. Catherine glanced over to make sure Father John was comfortable and saw that the old man's chin rested against his chest, his eyes closed. She decided there was no need to awaken him just to have him go and sleep elsewhere. Instead she turned to Andrew and said in a low voice, "Tell me what is on your heart, husband."

He spoke to the embers. "I am concerned about Gordon Goodwind."

"He has made a very strong impression upon me," Catherine replied. "And a worrisome one."

"I could accept the fact that he is an officer, a military man in all but name." Andrew shook his head. "But his only nodding acquaintance with our Lord is most troubling."

"And yet," Catherine said, speaking words for them both, "I feel unable to caution Nicole about this gentleman."

"I must agree." Andrew lifted his gaze to meet his wife's. "If Nicole does not ask, I feel I must trust her and her faith."

"And our God," Catherine added.

Andrew nodded. "Do you know, I also see in Gordon a man of deep personal conviction and strength. Not to mention an officer's commitment to his responsibilities. I sense that if ever he were to become a follower of Christ, he would be a convert heart and soul."

But Catherine's concerns remained fastened on her inability to speak with her daughter. "She is a woman," she said and could not hold the sadness from her voice.

"And what a woman," Andrew said somewhat bemusedly. "What a *lady*."

Father John drew his legs under him and used both hands to press himself upright. "You both worry overmuch."

"Father, I didn't realize you were awake."

"Only partly. But enough to know you two speak as parents of a maiden who has grown into a duchess." His eyes gleamed with good humor. "Did you not hear the man yesterday? All the world greets her as the viscountess now."

"Our daughter is not altered simply because Charles granted her some title," Andrew countered.

"What you fail to realize is that Charles gave her nothing." When Catherine rose to help him, John waved his daughter back into her seat. "She has *earned* this title. Charles simply recognized the lady Nicole has become."

Father John found a reason to chuckle in the silence his words caused. He moved slowly toward his bedroom as he said, "That young Gordon doesn't stand a chance. Between our Nicole and our God, you are looking at a marked man."

Chapter 5

It was a silent walk. Nicole felt too deeply for idle conversation. Gordon sensed her emotional turmoil and held to his silence as well. Step matched step as they traversed the wooded path that wound its way in and out of the tree growth and shrubbery that hid the deep bay from view.

Will my secret refuge be the same? Nicole found herself wondering. Everything in her world had suffered change. It was too much to hope that her hideaway had remained unscathed. The very thought was enough to make her hold her breath in fear, but also anticipation. They were only minutes now from the pinnacle where she and Anne had spent so many hours talking and praying together.

Even as that thought filled her, Nicole knew that the same pouring out of her soul to Gordon would fill a longing in her heart. Dared she? How would the gallant young man respond to her baring her innermost dreams and fears? She cast a quick glance his way but saw only the outline of a handsome face, eyes focused firmly on the trail ahead, mouth set in a somber line.

Nicole turned her eyes again to the footpath just in time to escape tripping over the bough of a fallen tree. Gordon had noted it. Already his hand had reached to her arm to steady her if she stumbled.

It would have been nice to walk the rest of the way with his hand protectively beneath her arm, but as soon as the danger had passed he dropped his hand once again. Nicole noted his distance as keenly as she had felt his presence just a moment ago, yet she dared not risk expressing such feelings. She was even hesitant about determining how he would respond to this place that to her somehow felt holy. Apart. A silent and vast sanctuary from a disturbing and tumultuous outside world.

Suddenly there it lay before them. The bay glistened in the sunlight. No ships of either commerce or war rested in the harbor or traversed the waters. Only a small fishing boat bobbed gently on the swell. No crashing waves crested and foamed. No dark clouds hung low with menacing gray. Nicole took a breath as if to draw in the scene before her. A silent prayer of thanks drifted heavenward from her heart. There was still one place of serenity left in her world. One place where she could feel safe and at peace. At least for the moment.

At the same time that she felt blessed to be allowed this gift, she also felt the stab of pain at the absence of Anne. Never had she missed her sister with such a sharp awareness. Tears gathered in the corners of her eyes, and Nicole turned her face into the gentle breeze, which always fluttered the leaves of the hillside aspens.

She became aware of a stirring at her elbow. Gordon had moved up beside her. He too was looking out over the bay, eyes half squinted against the reflective glare of the sun. "It's a picture," she heard him whisper and wondered whether he was indeed speaking to her or merely musing aloud. She had never seen his eyes so expressive of deep feeling, his jaw relaxed from all need to be vigilant. He too seemed to drink in the scene before him with a deep breath.

She turned toward him then, and her slight motion appeared to break his reverie. He flushed slightly as though caught exposing his inner thoughts.

Her eyes swung back to the familiar yet always changing scene that stretched before them. "Anne brought me here," she said in a flurry of words, partly to express her feelings for the place and also to remove for him any need to feel embarrassment. "It's very special. I felt it the moment I stepped out on the point. Before I returned to Nova Scotia as an adult, Anne often came here alone to sort out just who she was and what had happened in our lives. She knew, you see, long before I knew. That her parents were Acadians and that we'd been switched as infants. She had to accept that long before I did. I fully believed I was part of the Acadian community in the Louisiana bayous. My parents hadn't told me otherwise." She paused a moment, then said, "Our mothers, Catherine and Louise, had a special meeting place, too, on the high bluffs above their two villages."

Nicole found she couldn't go on and so fell silent again. She sensed Gordon move a step closer. Though she appreciated his comforting presence, she could not make herself look at him. After a moment she gave a slight shrug and straightened her shoulders. "Who's to know which parents were right to tell or not to tell? Maybe they both were. Maybe God knew I would have fought against the knowledge, whereas Anne was more the one to accept things and work through it in prayer. It took me years to learn about the power, the inner peace, found in prayer." She faced Gordon and gave a small smile. "Grandfather used to come here with us. I suppose it has been some time since he's visited the point." Her eyes turned somber. "And I would imagine he has visited it for the last time."

Gordon touched her arm. "Would you like to sit down?" he asked, his voice low and solicitous.

With the words came further remembrance. Yes, sit down. They had often sat together on a makeshift bench created by God through nature. Was their bench also still in place? Nicole glanced to the spot and was glad to see it was just as she'd remembered. She pointed to it, saying, "Anne and I often sat there together. Sometimes we read the Scriptures, or prayed. Sometimes we talked for hours. Other times we just sat in silence, feeling the same thing but in different ways."

He took her arm and led her to the seat, then with a gloved hand brushed away from it the dirt and scattered leaves of the winter past. Nicole was relieved when, after a moment of staring out over the peaceful bay, he sat down beside her. His nearness brought unexpected joy— and a mingling of sorrow, for there was the realization that she secretly longed to share her life with this noble man sitting so close to her. But did she have any right to such intimate thoughts? She shook herself free of the troubling inner discourse and began to speak. She wasn't sure if the rushed speech was to distract her from her present pattern of thinking or to quiet the deep need to share her buried thoughts. She hoped that he might understand.

"After Anne left to marry Cyril I would come here by myself—when my loneliness for her became too much to bear. I have always felt that my prayers from here are more connected, more free to reach God." She looked upward as she spoke and raised a hand toward the blue sky. "The answer to my prayer for her is more at hand because He connects with her too. A triangle of love, in a way. I sense her prayers for me as well. It gives me strength."

She watched as Gordon turned to her and nodded. His face had softened. No longer was he the full British officer—eyes ever alert in duty or danger. He was simply a man intent on hearing and understanding. She could read it in his eyes. It both thrilled and frightened her.

Gordon seemed to be deeply affected by her sharing so much of herself with him and in such an intimate way. He turned toward her again. "Nicole, I . . . you must know how I have come to feel about you. I know this might not be the proper time to express—"

"I fear you are right," Nicole said, cutting off his ardent words. She sprang to her feet. "This is not the proper time for any further lingering. Mama will be awaiting our return. I promised to help her."

She bit her lip. Why had she spoken so hastily? Just a moment before she had hoped to hear Gordon express his love. Yet the very thought of such an alliance made her tremble now. She felt caught in a riptide, pulled out to sea. Enjoying the lift of the underlying current, yet at the same time aware of the dangerous power that swept her helplessly beyond her willingness to think clearly. This was how she had felt when Jean Dupree had spoken words of love. So overcome with waves of emotion that she could barely discern her own mind. Her feminine heart yearned for marriage—a home. A man with whom to share her life. Surely God had included that in His plan for her life. But was the man to be Gordon Goodwind? She must be careful not to rush God's plans. She had heard Gordon's words to her father; they had troubled her heart. She could not—dared not—give her heart to a man who didn't know her Lord. Yet she felt a hesitancy to voice an outright refusal to his suit. She wanted to throw her love, her life, totally into his hands, to share the joys and the struggles that might lie ahead. For she was keenly aware that, in spite of all her resolve to hold steady and not let her heart lead the way, she loved him.

Another thought stirred her. He was, after all, an officer, and it appeared that their countries—his Britain and hers America—could soon be caught up in a full-scale war. A war in which, unless God intervened, even Gordon would be forced to take sides. Nicole realized she couldn't bear to lose him to either side of the conflict.

Silently Nicole prayed that her inner tears might not be revealed on her cheeks. She could not share her tumultuous thoughts with the man beside her. *Oh, if only Anne were here,* her heart cried. *Perhaps she could help me sort out my feelings.* But then she reminded herself that her best counsel would be found in prayer. *Be patient,* an inner voice seemed to whisper, and Nicole felt her shoulders lift just a trifle. After drawing a deep breath, she turned to Gordon, who had risen from his seat now and stood next to her. She offered an arm in hopes of reclaiming the distance that had suddenly come between them. "Mama must be wondering what is keeping me," she said, attempting to keep her voice even.

Gordon cleared his throat, and she watched his eyes drift out over the bay one last time. A wind had come up. It stirred the water's surface into small waves and rocked the fishing boat back and forth. "Indeed" was his only reply. She noted that his jaw was firm again, and his eyes held the look of disappointment. But he managed a brief smile and accepted her arm, tucking it close in the crook of his own.

They began the walk back, closer in proximity than the outward trek had been, yet somehow Nicole felt they were now even more distanced from each other. Earlier he was about to express his deep feelings, and she had abruptly cut him off. Surely he must feel rejected. Perhaps shamed. But that was never her intent. She loved him. She knew it for certain now. Still, he had been right. This was not the time to speak of love. With a feeling of despair she wondered if it would ever be. Was this love like her other—not meant to be?

He helped her around the fallen branch again and then spoke for the first time since leaving the point. "I thank you for sharing your little bit of heaven with me. I feel more privileged than I can hope to express. It's a beautiful place and one I shall carry in my memory for a long time to come."

But it was more than the natural beauty I wanted to share, Nicole wished to object. *It was my heart.* But she could not speak the words. Not now. Not with him being so gallant. Not with the distance between them. Perhaps it would have been better if she'd not stopped him. If they both had been able to express their feelings openly. Even if they argued their different perspectives, at least then they would have voiced their views—cleared the air for further discourse. But it was too late now. The damage had been done, she chastised herself.

But would Gordon indeed have argued his point? He was a man trained by years of service, used to following orders and holding in check his own opinions, especially when he was in disagreement. It was the way of those long at sea to remain tactfully silent. Nicole felt a blanket of sorrow drape over her soul. She tried to push it aside, but even so it was hard to engage in any kind of small talk to break the awkward silence during the walk back to her parents' cottage.

In the days that followed, the tension between them persisted, even though Nicole could see that Gordon was doing his best to be an agreeable and helpful guest. He was courteous, ever ready to assist Catherine or share stories with John, and eager to help Andrew spade the garden or bring in wood for the fire. Nicole appreciated his congeniality, at the same time wondering if part of his desire to be involved with the others was to distance himself from her and any possibility of further misunderstanding. But that was not fair, she decided. He was more than proper with her as well, seeking often to be of assistance.

But Nicole was beginning to feel a familiar restlessness. There were questions about her future she must one day face, and being of the disposition she was, she wished to fling herself at them once and for all, to settle them so that life could go on.

Charles had entrusted her with a sizable estate and would certainly expect her to administer the estate's affairs. She did not want to disappoint him, nor could she deny that she had a certain curiosity to see just what it was she now could name as her own. She had never before owned property. It gave her a sense of satisfaction to know she was a landowner. What potential, what possibilities, were now hers?

So despite the rumors of increased animosities, despite Catherine's eyes turning dark with worry as this weighed upon her, despite Andrew's obvious pleasure at having her home again and Grandfather's enjoyment of having Gordon at his beck and call, Nicole could feel her restlessness driving her onward. She prayed for wisdom in presenting her plans to the other members of the household. There seemed to be no softening of the certain blow. So at length Nicole just plunged into the subject as she and her mother washed the evening dishes.

"I have put off my duty to Uncle Charles quite long enough," she began. "And I'm afraid that if I don't make the trip soon, then I'll be doing so without the protection of Captain Goodwind. He has been excused from his post for too long on account of me. I feel I mustn't detain him anymore."

She noted the quick rise of Catherine's head. The look of being caught off guard. The pain in her eyes in knowing she faced something she had been dreading, yet had no power or right to resist.

"I must make plans to travel to the estate in Massachusetts and put things in their proper order," Nicole explained, more to cover for her mother's distress than to give required information.

Still Catherine did not speak. She bent her head low over the pot she was scouring. Nicole wondered if it was a tear that splashed into the dishwater.

"I fear if we don't leave while the weather is still holding . . ." Nicole decided not to finish the thought. Her mother had always been averse toward traveling in foul weather. Surely this argument would hold some weight.

The silence continued for some minutes. When Catherine did speak, it was just one word: "When?"

"I was thinking tomorrow," Nicole answered slowly. "If we get an early start and it proves to be a fine day, we can almost make it back to Halifax. I don't care for days on the trail and appreciate even less nights so spent."

Catherine nodded without looking up. Nicole knew her battle was half won. Now she had but to persuade her father. She hoped he would offer no more resistance than her mother had.

In the end it was her grandfather who spoke his mind. "I don't know what you can gain by taking up land in an area threatened by war. I'd feel much better if you'd just take one of the homes here in the village and then stay put. It's not a bad way of life. Sure, folks might not pay much mind to your being a viscountess after the first flurry of excitement dies down—but you've always been accepted as one of us. What more can you ask than that? This title nonsense belongs to Britain. That's where it should be left." His voice sounded rather gruff as he finished, but Nicole stepped over and kissed his cheek. She was surprised to find it damp from a tear he'd tried to hide. Perhaps his words were merely his attempt to hold her close in his own way. She kissed him again.

"If all goes well, Grandfather, I won't need to be away for long," she consoled him.

"Won't be back in time to bid me farewell," her grandfather said even more gruffly. "I've already hung on for about as long as I can."

The words shook Nicole to the center of her being. She cast a quick glance toward her mother. From the slump of Catherine's shoulders and her melancholic countenance, Nicole could see that her mother agreed. *Would it be just Father who might be gone by the time Nicole returned, if indeed she ever returned?* That seemed to be the question in Catherine's eyes.

"You must join me at the estate," she hurried on, captured by the idea that had just come to her. "All of you. I'll send for you as soon as I've made things ready, put some staff in place. Oh, don't shrug it off, Father," she said to Andrew. "You've earned your rest. Surely a man isn't expected to serve his way into an early grave."

But Andrew still shook his head, sadness making him appear older than Nicole had ever seen him. "I'm afraid there may be no coming or going—for any of us," he said, and his voice sounded tired. "This war that's brewing is bound to divide, not join."

It was a frightening thought and one Nicole would rather ignore. She looked to Gordon for his support, but his eyes were on the tips of his borrowed house slippers.

"At least we have Reverend Collins," Andrew said. "Perhaps we can still send messages through him."

It was a ray of hope Nicole grasped eagerly. "Of course. I'll send word through Pastor Collins in Boston. He'll let you know when I am established; then we'll devise a way to have you all join us."

No one argued her leaving any further, though no one seemed inclined to continue the conversation either. Catherine rose with the excuse of helping her father to his bed. Nicole hurried to take his other arm. There was still a silence, a tension in the room she longed to dispel. She was glad she would be spending the remainder of the evening busying herself with preparations for her morning departure.

By the time she returned to the main room, the borrowed house slippers had been placed on the mat beside the door and Gordon's leather service boots were missing. She knew he'd left the cottage to make arrangements for their travel.

Chapter 6

The hills of Boston were still as bare as untilled earth, and the sky remained gloomy and leaden from the recently departed storm. Nicole stood on the ship's quarterdeck, there at Captain Gordon's invitation, and watched as their vessel was rowed farther into the mouth of the Charles River. They were hugging the bank closest to the city, and for good reason. On the river's northern bank stood a crude wooden fort, which flew what she had been told was one of the rebels' many flags. This one snapped and whipped in the biting wind, and on it she could make out what appeared to be a great snake.

As Nicole looked out toward the American fort, four of the garrison's guns boomed loudly, a foretaste of tempests to come. Three of the balls landed far short of their ship, creating a triple geyser in the slate gray water. The fourth skipped across the wave tops like a well-cast stone. Each time the ball hit, puffs of steam rose from the intensely hot metal, and the sound struck the ship's side with the deep thump of a giant wooden drum. To her astonishment the men all gave a great cheer, which was answered faintly from the distant shoreline.

"Stout English oak! I say, there's nothing like a solid ship of the line, no indeed, sir!" Their harbor guide was a young lieutenant from the English blockade, inflated with the importance of guiding a heavily laden supply vessel to safe harbor. "The rebels aren't half bad with their aim, I'll give 'em that. But they're no match against our oak hull."

"Not so long as we stay at the far bank, well out of range," Gordon murmured from Nicole's other side. But his words were tossed away by the wind, as intended. Clearly he had little time for the young officer, for he then added, "If you will excuse me, sir, I shall see to my vessel."

The lieutenant gave but a half bow at Gordon's passage. Not even the war could reverse the hostility between the Royal Navy and the merchant force. Gordon obviously took the young man's attitude as an affront. His jaw bunched tight, and he jammed his hat down against the rising wind with an angry fist.

Nicole asked the young lieutenant, "Do the American colonials have control of the region north of Boston?"

"For now, your ladyship. Cambridge Common is aswarm with rebels, but only for the moment. General Howe has just arrived to take back control of His Majesty's northern troops. He'll see to these rebels soon as the men are resupplied. You can mark my words on that."

When Gordon finally returned to the foredeck, he also asked, "How goes the blockade, sir?"

"Hard work, Captain. What with the storms and the winds blowing right their way around the compass. Howling like beasts of myths, with their teeth hanging clear and dripping from the yardarms all winter long. Ice long as my leg, we had. A month and more between supply vessels. Why, at one point the underdecks were down to boiling their belts for meat. Hard, sir. Very hard."

They had been caught by the blockade vessels, just as Gordon had predicted. It came just after daybreak, when three sets of sails had appeared to landward, and together the trio had boomed out a full cannonade of warning. Instantly Gordon had laid his ship to, lowered all but his topgallants, and waited for the blockade commandant to arrive and inspect his papers. Because the wind and tide were against them, they had elected to be rowed in so they might remain well away from the colonials' guns.

Nicole observed the far shore slide gradually by. The scene was brooding and far too cold for the first day of April. She wrapped the greatcoat tightly around her frame as she worried over the signs and portents greeting her arrival in Massachusetts Colony, the late-winter winds and gunfire from the people she hoped to call her own.

"My word," the young lieutenant exclaimed, "but it will be nice to plant my feet upon the soil again!"

Nicole turned to him. While the lieutenant was perhaps her own age, his unshaven cheeks and narrow features made him look more boy than man. "Have you been long upon the blockade, sir?"

"Next month marks a year, ma'am. And more than two months since my last landfall."

The lieutenant was clearly taken with the viscountess, for each time he addressed her directly his features would flush. "I say, how was England when you last saw her?"

"Much as here, cold and blustery. I left in November."

"Six months to make the voyage? You must have run into some heavy seas."

"Yes." She had no desire to recount her voyage, nor her recent departure from Nova Scotia. It still left an aching void in her heart. There was no telling when she would see her beloved parents again. And John was growing visibly older, not to mention Andrew's own frail health. No, she refused to permit herself to dwell on this. Nicole shook away the worries and the sorrow and said, "I understand I am to pay my respects to the garrison commandant."

"Indeed so, ma'am. No doubt he will be honored to host such a distinguished guest as yourself." He pointed out over the nearest rooftops to where a series of flags whipped back and forth. "The northernmost hill has been taken over by the city's garrison. Where General Howe is at the moment, I have no idea. But one of his aides will certainly—"

Suddenly a harbor signal gun fired a shot across the water, the wind sending a stinging spume of gunpowder and sulfur directly into Nicole's face. Signal flags raced up the harbor flagpole. Gordon barked a command, and the ship's bosun responded with flags of their own. Gordon leaned over the rail and shouted to the rowers, "Avast there! Heave to. Anchors away on my order!"

"I say," the lieutenant complained, "the longboats are under my command."

Nicole stepped away, having no wish to get caught up in the officers' conflict. She watched Gordon as he strode from one side of his vessel to the other, and she felt grateful for the company of this strong and trustworthy man. Once again she entered the unknown, marked with danger and uncertainty. It was good to have an ally she could call a friend, and perhaps more than that.

Why was it, then, she found it so difficult to confess her true feelings, even to herself?

"His lordship will be most distressed that he was not here to greet you personally, my lady." The colonel in charge of Boston's garrison headquarters was a portly, red-faced man in his forties, who went by the name of Grudge. From Nicole's first impression, the name suited him perfectly. "I shall dispatch a messenger posthaste to inform him."

It was a lie, she sensed, but could not fathom why the man would consider it necessary to speak false-hoods to her. Nor why it seemed the man spoke every sentence with unspoken slurs. "That will not be necessary,

Colonel," she told him. "I intend to travel onwards as soon as transport can be arranged."

"A lamentable decision for us all, my lady." He used two fingers to lift the ship's manifest. "If you will forgive me, Captain, it says here that your ship was intended to resupply the New York garrison."

"I was sent northwards for supplies. But her ladyship had hired my vessel, and she ordered me here." Her escort clearly shared her impression of the British colonel, for Gordon's tone held a certain guardedness. "I assumed that so long as the supplies came into British hands, my task was done."

"Of course, of course." Grudge squinted over the papers. "It says you carried no weapons or powder."

"That is correct."

"Armaments were hard to come by, were they?"

Gordon chose his words carefully. "We brought what we could, Colonel."

That had been their joint decision. Even before landing in Halifax, Gordon had warned Nicole that Britain ruled the high seas, which meant they would more than likely be caught by the squadron guarding the Boston harbor. Their ship was English; the manifest bore an English seal. What was imprinted upon their hearts was best kept a secret.

"I understand." Colonel Grudge's quarters were in what had once been a splendid stone manor on the harbor side of Beacon Hill. But the interior was stained yellow now with dirt and smoke and hard use, and an infantry battalion was encamped about the manor grounds. Through the open window blew the brisk wind, blasts of trumpets, the rattle of war drums. The officer behind the ornate rosewood desk appeared oblivious to it all. He ran his eye down the long list of transported goods, sniffed loudly, and said, "Well, all seems to be in order here. And as you are no doubt aware, your supplies are most useful to us at this time. We have just suffered through the most dreadful of winters, I don't mind telling you. I'll begin the off-loading immediately."

"There is the small matter," Gordon said politely, "of my payment."

"Upon my word, did I neglect that? Forgive me, sir." He sniffed once more, then shouted out, "Barnes!"

Instantly a narrow head and even more slender body popped through the open door. "Sir?"

"Prepare a requisition order for these materials." He offered his aide the manifest. "Then have a company of those navy chaps see to removing these goods."

"I'm sorry, Colonel Grudge," Gordon said. "But my own orders were most specific. I must request that payment be made in gold sovereigns."

Grudge squinted over his desk. "The British army's paper is quite good, sir."

"That may be. But I am commanded by the ship's owners to request hard currency."

The colonel looked at Gordon as if inspecting him, then said, "Barnes."

"Sir."

"Prepare a payment in sovereigns for our visitors." When his aide remained standing agog in the doorway, the colonel intoned, "That will do, Barnes." Once the young man had departed, the colonel inquired, "What are your plans now, Captain?"

"My superiors have ordered me to escort the viscountess to her holdings, then to present myself and my ship in New York."

"Her holdings. Yes. Of course. And just where might these holdings be, my lady?"

"I am told they lie close to the Massachusetts Colony's western border."

The news seemed to amuse the colonel. "Is that so? How interesting."

"I will be requiring a safe-conduct pass," Gordon said. "For myself, the viscountess, and my men."

The colonel paused in the act of reaching for his pen. "Your men, did you say?"

"Yes, sir. I shall require an escort for the lady's personal belongings." When Grudge seemed displeased with this news, Gordon continued, "They shall be drawn from my ship's company, of course. I won't be requiring any of those under your command."

"No, of course not." But the colonel remained vexed nonetheless. "Yes, well, that's as it must be, I suppose."

"Pardon me?"

"Nothing, Captain. Just affairs of . . ." His voice trailed off as he scribbled busily. He then lifted the candle at the corner of his desk and used it to melt the edge of the red-square sealing wax. When enough had dribbled onto the base of his parchment, the colonel applied the military seal. "That should see you through our lines and patrols with utmost dispatch."

"I thank you, sir." Gordon looked over the document, rolled it up, and stored it away. "Might I ask of any regions which we should avoid?"

"All of Massachusetts Colony lies firmly within the grasp of General Howe." The officer rose to his feet and gave them both a thin smile. "Now if you will excuse me, I must turn my attention to other pressing matters. Captain, my lady, I bid you a safe journey and good day."

The most trying hours for Nicole aboard ship had been those of the late afternoon. The ship's company was busy with end-of-watch duties, and the ceiling to her small cabin thundered with the rushing of wooden clogs.

An officer from Halifax and his wife were in the cabin

next door, on their way to a new posting farther south. But the young woman had not been much company since she was in the early stages of her first pregnancy and feeling poorly.

That day, as usual, Gordon's voice could be heard shouting orders to some far reach, though the frigid wind blew the words into indistinguishable fragments. Outside her small window Nicole could hear the creaking of ropes through stubborn winches as the ship's cargo got hauled up from belowdecks and sent over the side to waiting longboats. Men shouted and groaned beneath the loads, officers called back and forth, the bosun piped his signals, the men hurried about in obedience. Everyone was busy; all had important work at hand. Except for her.

Nicole had taken to using this period of the day for Bible reading and reflection. When all hands were on deck, there was little room for her. And although Gordon staunchly refused to say so, she knew she was rather in the way. So she sat in the folding chair, positioned so the light from her window fell upon the page, and pondered the words of Scripture.

Gordon's voice called out once more, and she found her thoughts following the course of this strong man. While he had said nothing directly, she was certain that if she asked, he would give up his life at sea to be with her on land. And yet still she wouldn't permit him to pay formal suit. It wasn't that she did not care for him. She did, and more deeply with each passing day. But try as she might, her concerns were not to be denied.

The overheard conversation Gordon had had with her father that Sabbath afternoon echoed through her mind. She looked down at the sacred book in her hands and knew Gordon did not share her faith. Oh, he had a certain interest in the Divine. Her father had said it best: Gordon preferred to keep God at arm's length.

Here in her cabin, surrounded by the sounds of several

hundred men hard at work, she found herself descending into a calm that offered a striking clarity. Nicole stared out her small window at the patch of frothy gray water. She laid her hand on the open page and gave herself over to a keenness of reflection she knew came from other than her own mind and heart. She loved Gordon. There was no questioning the fact. But she was forced to keep these emotions a secret.

The one other love of her life had been a scalding experience. Jean Dupree had also been a strong man, self-reliant and full of passion. But such passions could have a dark edge to them, hold a harmful appeal. At least for her. Nicole no longer ached for the man she'd left behind in the green Louisiana bayous, but the lessons were with her still. She had grown to live more honestly, to know herself well. She understood a part of her had been captivated by the sense of adventure, of danger, embodied in Jean Dupree.

A knock at her door drew her around. "Yes," she called.

Gordon opened her door without stepping inside. "The men have been hard at it," he told her, "and the off-loading is almost complete."

"That is excellent news. When can we depart for the interior?"

"Tomorrow if you like." He paused.

"I am most grateful for your company on this journey, sir," she said carefully, trying to keep her emotions in check.

"Miss Nicole, if you will allow me . . ."

She could tell he was on the verge of speaking his feelings, as he'd been before. "Which men will be accompanying us?" she hurried to ask.

The tension in Gordon's shoulders released with an explosive sigh. "Bosun Carter and I have selected a dozen of our best."

"Then I am certain no one shall be as safe as I," she noted with a polite smile. When he remained standing there, filling her doorway, she raised the volume from her lap and asked, "Would you care to join me in my devotions?"

"Ah. No, thank you. Will you be joining the ship's officers for dinner?"

"I would be happy to do so."

"Until then." He bowed stiffly. "Your servant, ma'am."

Nicole winced at the force Gordon put to shutting the cabin door. She stared at the scarred wooden surface for a long moment, then whispered softly, "If only you could see how my heart yearns for you. If only you could know what is required."

Chapter 7

The next day it was well past noon before the knock was heard at the door. And it was the bosun who opened it, not Gordon. "Your pardon, my lady. The captain sends his regards and asks if you are ready to begin."

"Since early this morning," she replied, pointing to the one remaining trunk. "That is all I have left on board."

"Very good, my lady. The bosun's chair has been prepared for you."

The bosun was a stout barrel-chested man with a deeply seamed face. His strength was immense, and his voice loud as a cannonade. Yet he was a good and fair man, respected by the officers and men alike.

"Please be so kind as to use my name upon the journey ahead," she said to him.

Carter's features were stained the color of old tobacco from the sun and salt. Which made his teeth shine all the whiter when he smiled. "That I'll do, Miss Nicole."

"Thank you. And the rest of the men should do the same."

"Right you are, ma'am. Now if you'll just come this way."

Up on deck, Nicole found herself facing a phalanx of the ship's company. One of the young lieutenants doffed his hat and said, "We're all most dismayed to see you depart, my lady."

"Thank you, James." She lifted her voice and said, "Thank you all. I count each of you as a friend, and consider myself the richer for your company."

A quiet murmur ran through the gathering, the sound then caught by the biting wind and tossed overboard. But not before Nicole felt her heart swell from the unspoken accolade. She stepped to where the bosun stood holding the swinging chair at the railing. As she was winched up and over the side, the ranking officer commanded, "Present arms!"

As one, the ship's company removed their caps and stood bareheaded in the gloomy afternoon. Nicole searched the ruddy faces one more time and suddenly found herself heartsick over yet another journey into the unknown. While being gently lowered to the waiting longboat, she cried, "I shall miss you all!"

———— ✦ ————

To her surprise, the longboat did not head directly for the Boston harbor's main landing. Instead it skirted around three groups of fishing vessels and began slipping upstream. "Where are you taking me?"

"Captain's orders, ma'am," Carter replied from his place by the tiller. "We're to off-load away from prying eyes."

The tide and wind were both with them, so they made swift progress. They rounded the city's final hill into a region of unkempt marsh grass and stunted trees. The scene across the river couldn't have looked more different. Farmland stretched back as far as she could see. In the distance was a charming village. "What is that, please?"

"Cambridge is its name, ma'am, and depending on who

you're speaking with, it's either a den of thieves or a haven for all good men."

"I'm sorry, I don't understand."

"The American garrison is headquartered there, ma'am."

"An entire garrison?" Nicole peered across the water in astonishment. "But the colonel told us that all Massachusetts Colony was in British hands."

"Aye, I also was told. Which is strange, if you don't mind me saying, seeing as how we were met on our arrival with a cannonade from a fort taken from our redcoats just last year."

Now she could see a variety of flags waving over the village. A trumpet sounded tinny on the wind. "What does this mean?"

"You'll have to ask the captain that, ma'am. A good bosun learns to let the officers do the thinking and explaining." He pointed toward the shoreline, where three carts and a pair of horses waited for them. "Aim for the cut there, lads, and pull hard."

The men standing on the riverbank were no longer dressed as Gordon's seamen. Gone were the navy greatcoats and wooden clogs and buttoned trousers. They now wore high boots, slouch hats, and gray oilskin cloaks. Greeting the hard-faced travelers, Nicole said, "I shall not know any of you without your tarred pigtails."

The men grinned, and one seaman replied, "Wouldn't have cut it off for nobody but the captain."

"Been growing it for nigh on twelve years," another agreed.

Gordon directed the seamen bearing her trunk toward the nearest cart. "We can't risk word going out of a bunch of seamen escorting a titled lady inland." He raised his voice and said, "From this point on, it's *Miss Nicole* traveling with us, along to see her family. Nothing more."

Nicole nodded agreement.

"Aye, that's why the men vied hard for the chance to come along." Gordon led her to a chestnut mare tethered to the back of the cart. "This filly here has the gentlest mouth of them all, or so it seemed upon first impression. I assumed you would want to ride."

"Yes, and she's lovely." Nicole stroked the mare's neck. "I'm sure we are going to be best friends."

She held her other comments until the company had mounted and traced their way through the boggy forest to join the road, for Gordon showed a marked impatience to leave Boston behind them. The route was well traveled, with mounted British troops rattling past twice in their first few minutes. They also passed loaded wagons and carts of farm produce and several strings of high-spirited horses. Nearly all the traffic headed into town. Nicole watched the way Gordon studied the passersby and so asked, "Tell me what it is you see."

"A country on the move," Gordon said tersely. "Outlying communities moving to the safety of a garrison-held city. There will be fighting in the coming dry season, and these people are taking no chances."

"Which means the colonel failed to tell us the truth."

"Aye, my impression as well."

"But why would he lie?"

"I cannot say for certain."

"Then tell me what you think." When Gordon didn't respond, she pressed him. "Please. It cannot possibly be worse than my fears."

"Perhaps," Gordon said slowly, "the colonel heard of my brothers."

Nicole recalled from their seaborne conversations that Gordon's two older brothers were both now serving as officers in the army of Virginia. "Is that likely?"

"I cannot say. But it is a more appealing notion than the other."

"Which is?"

"That the colonel wished for us to hurry along so he might have us intercepted and the gold stolen from us."

Gordon's tone had turned bleak. "Gold is quite scarce, so I never expected to be paid in full with sovereigns. Half would have been acceptable. Three-fourths more than adequate as far as our shipowners are concerned."

"You're saying, then, that Colonel Grudge wished you away for some reason."

"Aye, that is my thinking."

"Where is the gold now?"

"On its way to London. The shipowners' bank has a Boston office. They were only too delighted to accept a sack of good English sovereigns. They confirmed my suspicions. It's rare for His Majesty's procurers to be handing out gold to inbound traders."

"Perhaps the colonel needed your supplies so desperately he was in no position to bargain."

"Perhaps. But until we know better I shall sleep with one eye open, and we will post a double bevy of guards."

But their way remained clear, their progress steady. Even the weather turned in their favor. They slept the first night in the lee of a farmer's barn and awoke to find the bitter wind and scuttling gray clouds to have dispersed with the dawn. A gentle breath rose from the south. The sky was a light blue, and all the world seemed impatient to embrace a newborn spring. From the farmer's wife they bought a morning's feast of freshly churned butter, baked bread, and still-warm eggs. Not even Gordon looked to be adhering to his own warning to keep a sharp eye out for trouble.

The only sign that the region might not be facing another normal planting season was how sparse the traffic had become. By midday they had the road to themselves, and traffic didn't begin picking up again until they had reached the outskirts of Bedford. They made their way around the town, and just a half hour later were again traveling alone. Twice they spotted farmers off in the distance, plowing behind teams of oxen. But other than this, the world seemed trapped in seclusion.

There was no clear transition point, either. The farther they ventured from Boston the clearer the fact became that this land was firmly in the American colonials' hands. The smallest hamlet flew a rebel flag, either that of the Constitutional Congress or the newer one of white stars over a blue field, partly framed by red and white stripes. Nicole thought this flag to be very jaunty, far nicer than those with guns or snakes or symbols of war.

At lunchtime Gordon buried the British safe-pass deep inside one of the chests. In its place he pocketed the official document given to Charles by the Constitutional Congress, confirming Nicole's ownership of the lands in western Massachusetts. Still they saw no soldiers and very little sign of conflict, just the empty road ahead and behind.

Toward evening of the third day, as they were closing in on Leominster, the wind shifted back to the north and the skies grew steadily darker. Gordon announced that the town appeared safe enough for them to risk lodging in an inn, and Nicole did not complain.

By the time they arrived at the village square, the temperature had dropped by half and a misting rain was pelting them hard. Even the horses seemed dejected, with their ears lying flat and their flanks shivering. The innkeeper's wife led Nicole upstairs to a comfortable front room, while the men saw to the horses and guards to the carts. Nicole hadn't realized how weary she was until a little while later when she rejoined the men for dinner and almost fell asleep over the hearty beef stew. But hunger kept her eyes open and her hand in motion, though she saw little else besides the bowl in front of her.

From his station on her right, Gordon leaned in close and said, "Are you attempting to ignore me?"

Nicole started from her half sleeping. "Forgive me. I am exhausted."

"I have spoken to you three times."

"I did not hear a word. I apologize. The road—"

"Will there never be a moment when we might speak together more intimately?" Gordon had pitched his voice low enough so that the words reached only her ears.

It was strange how, in the space of two heartbeats, she could go from a state of near slumber to as awake as she had been in weeks. "Most certainly."

"I would like to know when. The end of our journey is just ahead of us." Idly Gordon rolled his spoon back and forth between his fingers. "I will deliver you to your estate, then return alone to my ship. That is, unless . . ."

She knew he waited for her to ask, *Unless what?* But she could well imagine the response, and it was something she would rather not hear. "I find it most difficult to speak of the future, as it lies both tender and heavy upon my heart."

Gordon turned in his seat so as to face her squarely. "It is precisely this tenderness which I deeply desire to know better."

Nicole had no choice but to get up from the table. "I thank you for your company," she said, then raised her eyes and voice both. "I bid you good evening, gentlemen. Captain, I must get some rest now."

Gordon neither stood nor offered a polite farewell. Her last impression before leaving the room was of Gordon morosely spooning the remnants of his meal.

Nicole returned the innkeeper's good-night and climbed the stairs with a heart in turmoil. How she would so like to do as Gordon wished and reveal to him her feelings. How desperately she wanted him to stay. To remain on the estate and help her face all the unknowns of this volatile time. To become the man she could give herself to fully.

Yet her fears clamored more loudly than her longings. Nicole prepared for bed, her mind a litany of doubt and dismay. She was afraid of opening her heart further. In fact, she was terrified she had already gone too far. Feeling beset by her earlier mistaken love with another who had in similar fashion moved resolutely against the tides of faith, she wondered again whether some flaw in her nature drew her to one who knew not her Lord.

It seemed as though she had scarcely laid her head on the pillow before dreams swept her up and away. But there was little rest in this slumber, and no peace. For there in the dark her room was invaded by the presence of Jean Dupree, the Acadian she had loved so deeply, yet who was so wrong for her. The man reached across distance and years both and leered at her. In her half slumber Nicole cried out and heard herself do so, for the man of her past had found a way to break through her shield of faith. She awoke to find herself weeping, realizing then it wasn't Jean who had assaulted her but her own weakness.

The bitterness of her past mistakes, the pain of many trials, the fear of revisiting the hardships of her youth—all this remained with her and formed the doorway through which Jean had entered. Nicole lay in the dark and tried to stifle her sobs. She rose from her bed to kneel and pray for the strength to carve a new beginning for herself.

She clenched her hands together with the fervor of one who realized she had no answers of her own. No answers, and not nearly enough strength. "O dear God," she wept, "bring Gordon to his knees so he forms a new and true commitment to faith, whatever might come of my feelings for him. Show me if he is the one for me. Please, I beg you. Let this love be real and good in your eyes. But if it is not to be, please make that clear to me. And hurry, Father. There is so little time left. Please, I beg you."

Chapter 8

The weather remained unpredictable, with one day's wind blowing down winter from the north, and the next a warmth that bound them to a fairer season farther south. The land itself proved most agreeable, gentle rolling hills and large fields surrounding orderly farms. Nicole and her companions forded streams and creeks constantly, often catching glimpses of fish jumping out of the clear-running water. On the fourth day the south wind blew so kindly they traveled with oilskin cloaks rolled up and tied behind their saddles.

That afternoon, as they were passing around Templeton, a cadre of mounted men rushed over the edge of the road and crowded in tightly around the group.

They were unlike any soldiers Nicole had ever seen before. They held themselves in military fashion, with well-oiled arms at the ready as they circled and hemmed them in. But they were also a ragtag bunch, wearing homespun and stiff tricornered hats and patched trousers. Their officer was no different. Nicole recognized him only from the way he arranged his men with hand signals, then ordered their group sharply, "Hands where I can see them, gentlemen! And make no sudden moves if you care to observe another sunrise."

"We travel in peace," Gordon told him, showing his empty gloved palms.

"I'll be the one deciding that." The officer set his long-bore rifle across his saddle and demanded, "Now just who might you be, and what is your business here?"

"I have papers in my pouch that will explain."

"Mind you draw them out slow and easy."

Gordon untied his pouch and took out the folded document. He announced loud enough for all the surrounding men to hear, "It bears the seal of your own Constitutional Congress."

A murmur ran through the American soldiers as their officer inspected the document. "Why, so it does," he agreed. He read further on, then aimed his gaze at Nicole. "You are Miss Harrow?"

"You are addressing the Viscountess Lady Harrow," Gordon corrected.

The officer appeared unimpressed. "We don't hold much to royal titles in these parts."

"That is good to know," remarked Nicole. "For neither do I."

The officer's eyes glimmered. "We've had our fair share and more of high muckety-mucks come parading through here, putting on airs and waiting for us to offer the bended knee."

"I have met many such," Nicole said. "And don't cotton to such myself." She felt Gordon's quick look at her choice of terms.

"One man, one vote, that's our motto," their captor continued. "And none stand higher than the rest."

"I am liking this fair land all the more for knowing this," Nicole said.

The officer tipped his hat. "My name is Ida Sessions, ma'am. We're neighbors, in a manner of speaking. I own a parcel out Concord way."

"An honor and a pleasure, sir."

"Your father is this Charles Harrow fellow?"

Nicole could see Gordon bristle at the familiarity, but he held his tongue.

"My uncle," Nicole replied.

"We've word all the way out here of how he's been helping widows and orphans."

One of his men spoke up. "Know a good lady who's kept her land on account of his generous ways. Lost her husband and both her sons."

"I'm so sorry," Nicole said quietly, touched by the story of a woman whom she had never met. "The tragedy of war is simply too great to bear."

At the officer's signal, the men surrounding the group and blocking their way moved to either side of the road. "Beyond Millers Falls you'll need to keep a sharp watch for a band of renegade Indians. There's some as haven't declared for either side and have taken the troubles as a good time to loot the unwary."

"How stands the war?" Gordon asked.

The officer examined him carefully. "The lady is mentioned in this document, sir. But not yourself."

"Captain Gordon Goodwind, sir. Merchant navy. At your service."

"Are you holding to the British cause?" the officer wanted to know.

"I have two brothers fighting with the Virginia regiments."

Ida Sessions wasn't the least bit impressed by this. "I know more families than I can count who've been split by the terrors, sir."

"My own family," Gordon said cautiously, glancing toward his men, "has known no such calamity."

The officer appeared satisfied with Gordon's response. "Well," he said, "all's been quiet in these parts for five months and more."

"And elsewhere?"

"The Carolinas were attacked with regiments brought in by sea. But we're harrying them hard. We've a good man in command down south. Swamp Fox, he's called. General Francis Marion. Formerly with your forces. Perhaps you know him."

"I've not had the honor, no sir."

"No matter." The officer tapped his saddle with his reins. "The Harrow lands lie west of the Connecticut River Valley?"

"I believe that's right, sir," said Nicole. "I have the documents in my trunk."

"Not necessary, ma'am." He gave Gordon a sharp look and said, "There was considerable fighting out that way last autumn."

Gordon's jaw tightened. "Who is now in charge?"

"Hard to say."

Nicole watched as her escort gave a thoughtful nod and said, "I am in your debt, sir."

The officer backed his horse out of the way of their carts. "You know how rumors fly during such times."

"All too well," Gordon agreed.

"We have word that the British are planning a major assault in the early summer. They aim to retake all lands between Boston and New York."

"But those are cities on the sea," Nicole pointed out. "So we should be safe this far inland."

The officer kept his gaze steady on Gordon. "They are reported to be bringing troops down both the Hudson and the Connecticut Rivers."

Gordon gave a second slow nod. "Again, sir, I am most grateful."

Only after they had put the next row of low hills between themselves and the American troops did Nicole ask, "What did the officer mean by all that?"

Gordon's features looked forged from the experience

of war. His tone was more direct than he normally used with her as he said, "We shall know soon enough."

Their fifth day on the road dawned warm and utterly still beneath a sky quilted with drifting clouds. Nicole found herself drawn forward in eagerness, each hill becoming one ridgeline closer to their destination, each valley descending toward what could become her very own home.

She replayed in her mind numerous times the conversation with the American officer, especially how he had mentioned the good works of her uncle Charles. This is what she wanted for herself, a chance to use her position and wealth to add to the goodness she saw in this vast and verdant land. She wanted to seek out the needs and then help to fill them. Nicole shivered with anticipation at the thought. What finer life could she ask for herself than to be God's servant here in this great beloved land?

Millers Falls was as benevolent and peaceful as the day. The only change Nicole could see after leaving the village was how the farms became more widely scattered and the road less tidy. Twice the men had to dismount and maneuver the carts around gaping holes in the road.

But they noticed no signs of danger. Fortunately the brush had been cut well back from the road, so their vision remained clear. Even so, Gordon stationed men to either side of Nicole, and all rode with firearms at the ready. Yet there was little tension among the men, and the only surprise they had was when a trio of high-antlered deer sauntered across the ridge ahead. The deer were out of range, but the sight alone was enough to put them all in high spirits.

In late afternoon they began climbing the highest of

the hills. The rise was so gradual they could almost ignore the fact they were climbing at all. Then it grew increasingly steeper toward the ridgeline till it seemed they were riding directly into the setting sun. The light blazing from the cloudless sky was so fierce Nicole had to shield her face with the brim of her wide bonnet. She felt she was sweltering beneath her layers of clothing.

Because she was squinting, she hadn't realized they reached the crest until the men in front of her halted. She shaded her eyes, then added her gasp to their astonished murmuring.

There in front of them spread one of the loveliest vistas Nicole had ever encountered. Far below, the Connecticut River cut a broad swath through a valley a good two miles in width, bordered on either side by great forests. Here and there were precise squares cut by neat little farms, most of which nestled in close to the road that snaked down one side of the valley and up the other. In the far distance Nicole could make out glimmers of even higher hills, perhaps mountains. Their white peaks shone against the sunlit horizon like crowns of welcome. Nicole felt a surge of delight at the thought of living in such a valley.

As their path wound downward, Gordon drew them into the front corral of a farmhouse just north of the road. Several of the men spoke quietly among themselves before Carter finally said, "Begging your pardon, sir. But would you be planning to stop here?"

"Oh, we can't possibly be!" Nicole protested. "There are hours left of daylight!"

Her words seemed to be lost on Gordon. He dismounted and said, "I thought it best to inquire about inns and the road ahead."

The bosun reached for Gordon's horse, then said, "Sir, the men and I, we was wondering. Could you ask the house who owns the fallow land hereabouts?"

Gordon cast a thoughtful glance to his crew, then out

over the surrounding valley. "Yes, all right."

He called a greeting to the house and approached with his hands outstretched. Nicole was taken aback by his caution, but the men were far more interested in the lovely valley than their captain's demonstration of peaceful intent.

The men turned about only when the farmhouse door cracked open and a gun barrel poked through the space. Gordon halted on the bottom step and stood as he was, palms out and away from his sides.

When the farmer didn't come out any farther and Gordon stayed planted, Nicole turned and whispered to the bosun, "Why is the man in the house being so cautious?"

"Hard to say, ma'am." Carter's expression was worried. "My guess is that there's been other visitors of late, and some were flying false colors."

Before Nicole could ask what he meant, Gordon doffed his hat to the farmer and wheeled about. As he approached them he said tersely, "There's an empty farmhouse a quarter mile farther down the road and with a good well, so says this man. We'll overnight there."

"Oh, can't we travel on just a bit more than that?" Nicole implored.

"I don't wish to risk being caught in the open come dark," Gordon replied.

One of the men nudged his horse closer. "Pardon, sir, but did the man happen to say anything about who owns all this land?"

"As far as he knows," Gordon said, mounting his steed, "the land belongs to whoever clears it."

A ripple of disbelief ran through the men, and many twisted and looked again out over the lush green valley. "The land's here for the taking?" one said.

Gordon gave the sailor a stern look. "You signed on for the entire voyage, remember that."

"Aye, sir." But the man couldn't help but give the impressive expanse of open land another look. "There's no harm in thinking ahead, though, is there, sir?"

Once they were encamped in the derelict farmhouse and their supper was cooking in the crumbling fireplace, Nicole moved up alongside Gordon. "Did the farmer happen to say anything about my estate?"

Gordon continued to survey the surrounding fields, his face impassive but with an unsettled look in his eyes.

"Gordon?"

"My dear," he said softly, "some things are best left for the light of day."

Chapter 9

It had become Nicole's habit to hold a prayer time with the dawn. The men were good seagoing stock and accustomed to Sabbath services, and they normally tolerated her morning devotions with quiet good humor. Today, their sixth on the road, was different. The men moved about with grim watchfulness, as though sometime during the night they had caught whatever it was that held Gordon's features in such austere lines.

They breakfasted in silence and then continued on their way, four men riding close to the left and right of Nicole. But other than their own countenances, there was neither danger nor gloom overshadowing the day. The closer they came to the river, the more the air warmed, until it seemed to her as if the very best of summer lay trapped within this glorious valley.

A battered flat-bottomed ferry had obviously spotted their approach, for the two ferrymen had roped and rowed their way across from their shacks on the opposite bank. Planks were laid down, and the wagons eased gently onto the rough-hewn deck. Only one of the horses balked at the prospect of stepping onto the floating platform. The ferry skipper, a bandy-legged man with a perpetual squint, whipped off his neckerchief and bound it over the horse's eyes. As soon as the steed quieted, he personally led it on board. He tied the steed to the railing and signaled to his mate, and they began hauling hard on the ropes. Neither ferryman said a single word, other than to name their price. When Gordon asked him about the road ahead, the man spit a stream of brown tobacco juice over the side and turned away.

Once away from the landing area on the other side, the road soon deteriorated. It had clearly once been a well-laid lane but was now overgrown and badly rutted from the winter rains. Watching the men dismount a fourth time and manhandle the wagons through a series of deep cuts, Nicole protested, "Why do they not keep the roads in better condition?"

Gordon wiped his brow before saying, "My guess is, the local landowners are responsible for keeping up the stretch that runs through their holdings."

"Well, then. That should make it even more simple to find the one responsible."

Gordon started to give her a reply but instead commanded sharply, "Close in on all sides. And check your powder!"

Nicole looked around as the men hastened to obey. "Are there Indians?"

"I hope not," said Gordon.

"Then what is it?"

"At this point," he said, "I fear it could be almost anything."

The man's taciturn answer left Nicole unable to ask anything more. But as they crested the next ridge, impatiently she scouted to every side, searching for some sign they might be approaching the Harrow holdings. A town perhaps, or farmers tilling their fields. Anyone they might hail and ask the exact location of the estate.

The summit revealed yet another beautiful vista, of rolling hills and higher peaks beyond. In the fresh morning light the entire region held the promise of new seasons and quickening growth. The air was sweet and filled with birdsong. In the undergrowth to her right, Nicole spotted her first spring flowers, a carpet of bluebells stretching into the distance.

But there were no people.

They passed farm after farm, all of them vacant. After hailing the first three, Gordon silently led them by the rest. Some were obviously abandoned, with broken shutters and jagged holes where doors and windows had once been. Others looked as though the family had merely stepped out for a while. Except that the fields were unkempt, the barns empty. Fence railings had fallen into disrepair, and the pastures contained no stock. No cattle lowed, nor sheep grazed. Despite the day's sunlit beauty, the valley through which they moved turned oppressive with the absence of humankind.

And when the next valley revealed yet more empty dwellings, Nicole could bear it no longer. "Tell me what you have learned," she said to Gordon, her voice low.

"Nothing definite," said Gordon, "so perhaps—"

"Please, I must know. Tell me now. Where is the estate?"

He sighed. "We have been traveling by Harrow land since the river."

She reined in her horse and stared at him.

"Everything north of the road is yours, if what the farmer told me last night is in fact true."

"But . . . where is everyone?"

"You heard the American officer the same as I." He stopped a moment, then continued carefully, "Both the British and the Americans have taken and held this region."

"But what does that mean?" When he didn't respond, she said, "What of—what about the estate?"

"We shall see soon enough," he replied, obviously

keeping his tone even, then raised his hand to the company. "Forward!"

———— ✿ ————

Rather than the joy she expected to feel, the thrill of coming to a place that could hold her future, Nicole approached the tall gates with dread. They appeared just as the documents prepared by Charles's lawyer had described. The manor Charles had arranged to be built, yet had never seen himself, was situated on top of a rise, the lawyer had informed her, commanding views in every direction. Stone gates had been erected to match those at the entrance to Harrow Hall in England. As soon as she caught a glimpse of the gates, Nicole knew. Although the manor itself, hidden around a forested bend in the rutted track, was not in sight, she knew. She wanted to tell Gordon to turn back now. But her trembling mouth was unable to form the words.

The company entered through the gates, pausing momentarily to stare blankly at the makeshift huts made from tree boughs and tattered cloth that leaned against either stone pillar. The track had once been a fine broad lane but, unkempt now, it was overgrown with weeds. The wagons creaked and bumped in protest as they moved forward.

To both their left and right, wherever there was sufficient open land, remnants of army camps could be seen. Tent poles were set up in orderly lines, with ashes from countless campfires lined off into the distance. Then the forest closed in. Though the day was still brilliant and sunny and warm, Nicole found herself fighting off tremors of a deep chill, as if her very bones were clenched in the cold of misfortune.

They reached the bend, and the sunlight danced upon

the pasture beyond the woodlands. Nicole shut her eyes. She gripped the pommel with both hands, lowered her head, and prayed. More a mute cry than anything rose to the level of words. A brief few heartbeats long, a desperate appeal for strength.

Feeling a hand on her arm, she lifted her head to find Gordon drawn up alongside her. His hand settled there, while his gaze continued to scan the landscape. Nicole reached over and laid her hand on his. No words would suffice just then.

They exited the forest, and looking up, Nicole could not hold back the cry of heartbreak.

Broad fields stretched out in front of them, sweeping up a gentle slope where a once-majestic manor home had been built at the hill's top. The manor was burned and gutted. In fact, all the farms and outbuildings visible in every direction had been reduced to ashes and ruin.

Carter spoke for the first time since entering the estate. "There's been a battle here, sir."

"More than one, I warrant," said Gordon. "You men, keep together. Prime your muskets. Ready your arms."

Nicole still gazed up at the roofless manor, gripped by a sight she longed to wipe from her vision. Here and there blackened walls rose from the cloak of ashes, giving hints of its former stateliness. The northern face was the one most intact, with three tall, domed windows yet standing, though most of the glass was missing. A pillared veranda extended outward toward them, the columns now appearing like blackened teeth.

She was alerted to the danger by Gordon's grip tensing until it nearly cut off the flow of blood in her arm. Then he dropped his hand to his pistol and ordered, "Look lively there."

A flitting shape slipped by one of the remaining windows. Just seconds later Nicole saw a man drop from the rear of the house to the ground and dash away to her right, using the high grass for cover. Two more followed.

"Another moving off to the left," muttered Carter. "And two more."

"Turn the wagons about, and right sharp," Gordon commanded. He then raised his voice and hailed the house, "We mean no harm, maties! We are looking for cover against the night and nothing more!"

A voice from inside shouted back, "You'd best be looking elsewhere, while you still can!"

"Aye, that we will." To Carter, he said, "Have sharpshooters at the ready."

But this is my home! Nicole wanted to call out, to shriek at the heavens. This is *home.*

"Hurry up with those wagons," Gordon hissed.

"They're moving into range," Carter said.

"Give a warning shot near as life's breath to the front man," Gordon ordered.

Nicole had seen the bosun in action before. He was uncanny with a musket, able to drop a wild turkey in full flight from a hundred fifty paces. Without another word, Carter raised the musket to his shoulder, squinted down the long barrel, and pulled the trigger. There came the brief flicker of the powder charge catching, a pause, then the roar of smoke and flame. The bullet blew the hat off a man Nicole hadn't even noticed before. The soldier yelped and hugged the earth. Carter quickly handed the musket to the man at his right and accepted another one with a fresh charge.

"We're armed and at the ready!" Gordon hollered. "And that was the only warning we'll fire. Either call back your men or face your last battle here on this earth. Once we start, we'll end by rushing the house and finishing the lot right off!"

There was a long pause, then they heard, "Fall back!" When none moved, the voice from within the house cried, "You heard me! Retreat back to quarters!"

94

At this a group of ragtag men slowly stood from the waist-high grass and began making their way back to the house.

Gordon shouted, "You three there by the chicken coop! Get up or we'll bury you where you lay!"

Just as the trio jumped up and ran back toward the manor, a sailor reported, "Wagons turned and ready, sir."

"Off with you, then. You too, Nicole. We four will stand and guard your backs. When you reach the gates, Carter, fire one round."

"Aye, sir. Let's go, lads."

Nicole didn't object. She had seen enough. Whatever promise these lands and this house had once held was now defiled by the onslaught of war. With heart heavy, she moved to the position pointed to her by the driver, riding between the second and third wagons. The drivers stood on their seats, the reins flipped around one forearm while their hands held loaded muskets.

The forest felt even more stifling upon her departure. When they rode past the gates and the last driver fired into the air, Nicole could not quell the tears. It seemed to her that gunshot aimed directly for the center of all her fragile, broken dreams.

Chapter 10

At Gordon's insistence they pushed the animals hard and traversed the entire distance back to the Connecticut River without halting. Outriders trotted ahead and behind, staying just within sight of the main party. Gordon had ordered his men not to fire further warning shots, no shot across the enemy's bows. They were dealing with deserters, and such men knew no law save their own. If his men spotted any movement at all, they were to attack.

The sun was but a final glimmer over the western hills when they arrived at the riverbank. Gordon refused to accept the ferryman's argument that night was coming. He doubled the payment for an immediate crossing. The animals were tired and surly and had no interest in boarding. Which meant each had to be blindfolded and led onto the platform, with men heaving on the wagons to help the loading. By the time they reached the other bank, dusk was a thick gray-blue shroud over everything, and all were puffing with exhaustion. Even so, Gordon cajoled and pressed and got man and beast moving once more. Nicole knew his goal was to reach a spot off the trail, one where they couldn't be seen by any trackers who may have been sent out after three overburdened wagons.

The climb up the steep road toward the ridge seemed endless. Nicole's horse stumbled from fatigue. She decided to climb down and walk. She was herself soon blundering over unseen rocks and crevices. Pacing alongside the wagons, the men pressed in to push and shout and shove whenever the horses showed the least bit of hesitation. Their way was shrouded in darkness. No light burned from any window Nicole could see, nor was there a moon to burnish the road ahead. Reluctantly Gordon lit a few brands, but the torches only served to heighten the inky blackness all around them.

She found herself slipping into a state of half slumber, walking and dragging on the reins, yet somehow partly asleep at the same time. From the forests to either side, night creatures shivered and croaked and rustled. She heard vague whispers rise in her mind as well, indistinct murmurs from long-ago treks into the Louisiana bayous. She felt like a child again, seeking refuge.

Nicole didn't know how late it was when they finally made it back to the empty farmhouse where they had overnighted before. She knew nothing except how difficult it was to untie her bundle from behind the saddle. She felt guilty for not helping the others unsaddle the horses and tether them. She should also lend a hand with preparing a campfire and food. In the far-off distance of her mind, she registered the fact that she was ravenous. But for the moment it was all she could do to find a sheltered corner in the gutted farmhouse, spread out her blanket, sink down, and draw her cloak up over her head.

———— ✿ ————

She awoke hours later to a sound that was both familiar and totally alien. It took her a moment to realize the sound wasn't part of her nightmare. Then she heard it again and knew instantly what it was. Somewhere above her head, a mouse was scrabbling across the floor. The recognition was enough to draw her nightmare out into the realm of conscious thought, something she had not experienced since a little girl. Back then, in the hard times before her family had arrived in Cajun country, such waking dreams had been a common occurrence—as though her fears and childhood tremors were too great to keep within the world of dreams alone.

Nicole shifted beneath her blanket, and her movement was enough to send the mouse scuttling for cover. But the nightmare wasn't so easily dispersed. She knew now what she had been dreaming. It was one from her early days, that of a road without end. She and her family were walking, walking, walking. Without purpose, without hope. Just walking. And she knew once again the helpless fear she had known as a child, when all her family was deep in slumber and she had clenched the blanket with her hands and between her teeth, determined not to disturb her brother's exhausted sleep with her whimpers. Only now there wasn't a little brother sharing her blanket, so she didn't need to remain quiet. She could rise from the bed.

Quietly she stepped through the open doorway into the cold night. The wind had switched to northerly, and clouds robbed the night of even starlight. For once, Nicole did not mind the chill. Considering her feelings at the moment, it seemed fitting to sit on the porch's edge and feel a cold that coincided within and without.

She leaned her head against the railing. She was so tired, so very tired, and not just from the day's interminable march. She was weary in her bones and heartsick. She had so wanted a place where she could settle down and rest and plant roots and grow.

The thought caused her to open her eyes once more. She heard the murmur of the night watchman somewhere back of her, smelled the smoke, and listened to the horses' sleepy snorting. She had never consciously wished for such a thing before. Often she had wondered if ever she would find for herself the place where she belonged, but it had always been a vague yearning. Something felt mainly because she could see how important it was to others around her—Anne, Charles, Andrew and Catherine, Henri and Louise. All were so deeply grounded in the places they called home. To them, this need was so vital it required no words. For her, it was always more mysterious, something she suspected she'd been born without. Yet now, in her fatigued state, the need was a hunger more fierce than her empty stomach. She *needed* a place that was hers for all time. She needed a *home*.

Her aloneness and vulnerability nearly overwhelmed her. Nicole shut her eyes and sent another wordless plea lofting heavenward. The inner cry was filled with fear and with the need for her Father's protection.

There was a long moment of nothing but the rising wind and the quiet night sounds. Then Nicole sensed the presence of another, one not seen with her eyes so much as felt in her heart. She found herself utterly convinced that Henri Robichaud, the father she had known all her life, was awake in this dark night and thinking of his daughter, praying for her. The loving protection he had always offered her was there with her now. The answers to all her questions may not be found during this harsh hour, but still there was enough comfort that she could slip into easy, dreamless sleep.

They departed with the dawn.

Gordon didn't relax his vigil until they were again on the other side of Templeton. On the outbound journey, this stretch of road had seemed far too empty and strangely hostile. Now, after the desolation they had seen on the river's opposite bank, this region felt like a heaven-sent haven.

The weather remained draped in cold and wind and veils of misty rain. Nicole looked so fragile to Gordon, as she slumped beneath an oversized oilskin, the hood drawn so far forward he could see her face only when directly in front of her. Even then her eyes remained shrouded and distant.

The only time she seemed to be aware of the present was in the mornings and evenings, when she pulled the worn Bible from her saddle pouch and pored over its pages. She still invited him to join her. Gordon's affections were such that he was tuned to every nuance of her lovely voice, with its soft French accent rounding the words. He heard the quiet desperation behind her request. He didn't understand it, but he heard and took note of how intensely she desired him to read with her.

But he could not. He could not and remain honest with himself or her. And his feelings were so deep now he couldn't see himself ever acting in less than a forthright manner toward her— particularly concerning her faith, which was such a vital component of her life. Much as he would like to see their relationship develop to where he could press his suit, he could not do so through false means. He loved her too much.

But the truth was, he was sure her sort of faith had no place in his world. He cast these arguments back and forth in his mind over the long, wet ride back to Boston. He wanted a chance to tell her, but Nicole seemed lost within her own internal vistas, lost to all but the next stretch of road and all she had faced back there on her ruined estate. He didn't wish to quarrel, however. He wanted to tell her that he would give up his career and the sea both and help her rebuild. He would gladly aid her in establishing a new home, and a family and a lineage. Here. In America. He would even give up England. For her. If only she would lift her gaze and search his own and say she was ready to speak with him about such matters.

But Nicole did not speak save for the briefest of exchanges and her invitations to read and pray. And pray he would. Of course he was willing to do that, but not in the manner she sought. He was tempted to lie and do so out of necessity. But he would not yield. Honor and his growing love would not permit it.

Her sort of faith was too dependent, he thought. Too needy. Too *feminine*. A man survived in this world by counting on his mind, his strong right hand, his aim, his arms, and his few tried-and-true mates. Family also, if he was truly fortunate. The world was a place of woe and danger. Strength, determination, and ambition were what counted. Together with a proper respect for the cut of one's enemies. And there were always enemies. Always.

It was fine and good that she should practice her religion with such fervor. Noble even. But it wasn't for the likes of him. Unless she allowed him to address the issue fully and then be inclined to accept him as he was, he remained trapped, helpless.

Gordon felt a sudden burning urge to pound his saddle and rage at her, command her as he did his own troops, and insist that she hear him out then and there. But he immediately knew there was no hope for success in such a direct assault. He had come to know this woman well enough to be certain of that. So he tugged savagely on the reins and raced back to check on the outrider. A final glance over his shoulder told him that Nicole was completely unaware he had even left.

He lifted his face to the misting rain and felt the wetness cover him like cold tears. In all his days he had never felt so aggrieved. Or so helpless.

Chapter 11

Arriving at the alley by the harbor front was both comforting and tragically familiar. Up ahead Nicole glimpsed the same battered door leading to the hostel where she had stayed during her first journey northward from Louisiana. She could only hope that Pastor Collins—the wise old man with the gently piercing eyes—was still there to greet her. It would be reassuring to speak once more with the kindly pastor who had helped lead her to faith, and to be with someone who had known Andrew and Catherine. And yet as she approached the doorway, she couldn't help but reflect on how life had brought her full circle. In spite of the years and the miles and the struggles, she was still no closer to arriving at—at what? What was the goal?

Arriving in Boston, it had taken hours of searching to find a decent stable. Gordon had asked every British officer they passed until he'd heard several refer to the same place as trustworthy. For they wouldn't merely be leaving their horses and wagons there but also the valuables Nicole had brought from England. Gordon had argued with the stable owner to no avail. In the end they were forced to pay a staggering sum to stable the horses—more, in fact, than for a dozen rooms and meals at a neighboring inn during normal times. Once that was over, Gordon had insisted they use the mounts to travel to the inn. Just in case, he told Nicole. The city was extremely crowded, and he intended to ride around until a place was found where the men could all bunk down together. In such conditions, there was safety in numbers.

Nicole was midway down the alley before she realized that Gordon and the men were not with her. She turned back and asked, "Are you not coming?"

"Of course, of course." Yet Gordon continued to search the bayside waters a moment longer. "Forgive me. I cannot see my vessel."

"There's been such wind and storms, sir," Carter pointed out, his face aimed seaward as well. "They must've pulled the boat to a leeward shore."

"No doubt." Gordon peered down the shadowy lane. "You say there is an inn down this way?"

"A hostel and safety both," Nicole confirmed.

"You have been here before?"

"Some years ago."

"So before your time in England, I take it." Gordon chose his words carefully. "Even with the city's crowding of Loyalists, I am certain you can still find a place more fitting for a lady of means."

"That may well be," said Nicole. "Still, I would prefer to stay here."

She cut off further discussion by dismounting and proceeding to the doorway to ring the bell hanging above. Gordon waited a few moments, then quietly stood behind her.

They hadn't been standing there long when the door opened. A wide-eyed Reverend Collins stared at Nicole and exclaimed, "Saints above!"

The relief at seeing a familiar face and the delight with which the old man greeted her were almost too much for Nicole. She had to swallow an upsurge of emotion before responding, "Greetings to you, Pastor."

"My dear, I heard your voice through my open window." He pointed down the alley without taking his eyes off her. "Had I not just received a letter addressed to you, I would have thought I was hearing an angel. As it was, I could scarcely believe my good fortune."

"A letter? Here?"

"Two, in fact. One from Halifax, addressed in your father's hand. Accompanying that was one from a lady in England."

"Anne!" cried Nicole. "She has written! And it has arrived!"

"It has." The pastor gave the smile she remembered so well, shining with compassion and welcome. "Might I hazard a guess that you are in need of some good news?"

"Oh, sir, if only you knew. We have endured endless days of rain and mud and distant gunfire. This after a week of traveling west, only to discover that my home has been destroyed and is now occupied by deserters!"

"How tragic for you." If the old man failed to understand her trembling words, he showed no sign. Instead he reached for her hand. "Come inside and rest yourselves. All of you."

Only then did she realize she had forgotten to introduce Gordon. "Oh, please forgive me. It is all just too much. And with the letters . . ." She gestured to Gordon. "Might I introduce my escort and friend, Captain Gordon Goodwind."

"You are most welcome in my humble abode, Captain."

"An honor, sir." Gordon gave his stiff bow and asked, "Might you also have room for my men?"

"Of course, of course. Nothing fancy, mind you. But clean and dry—that much I can offer you all."

"If there's enough space for them to hang their hammocks and rest in safety, we will all be more than content."

The captain took a step back. "Now if you'll excuse me, first I will help see to the horses."

—————— ✿ ——————

Pastor Collins ushered Nicole inside. "Come in, my dear. Come in," he welcomed her.

Everything was as she remembered. The same stone-floored entrance gave way to the dining room with its long table and simple chairs. Beyond this was the hallway and then the pastor's small office. The same wooden cross hung on the wall, the same lead-paned window, the same clutter of books and papers. Nicole took a deep breath and could smell the familiar mixture of dust and candle wax. She said softly, "I am back."

"Yes, and what a joy this is for me, I cannot begin to say. Will you have tea? Are you hungry?"

"Tea would be wonderful, if it's not too much—"

"Nothing is a bother, my dear. Nothing. Sit yourself down. Here, read these while I see to the tea." Pastor Collins led her to the room's only padded chair, handed her the letters, then hurried out.

The two missives were bound together with blue ribbon and sealed with wax. She released the bond and first inspected the letter from her father. She felt his closeness through her fingertips, the warmth of his smile, the force of her mother's love. She slipped the letter into her pocket to be read a bit later and focused her attention on Anne's letter. Now her hands began to tremble, so much so she feared tearing the delicate paper as she broke the seal. Nicole laid the letter in her lap. The writing was so familiar she could almost hear her sister's voice. "Oh, Anne," she murmured.

Only after she'd composed herself did she pick up the letter and break the seal. Weeks of damp and briny air had turned the paper fragile as tissue. She held it close to the candle, her eyes capturing every word.

"Your sister wrote me such a lovely letter," Pastor Collins told her, returning with the tea. "She wrote to me as though we had been friends for years."

"Forgive me, sir, but this is the first letter I have received from her since leaving England. The conflict—"

"Yes, yes, of course. I understand completely." He set the cup down on the small table at her side. "You rest yourself here as long as you like, my dear. We can talk later."

In places the words had streaked and run, as if even the script itself had suffered from the turmoil. But Nicole knew her sister's words even before she read them. The solace they brought was tinged with regrets, though. The span of time, the vast distance, the fact that their countries were at war all added to the bittersweet feelings swirling within.

Having scanned the contents, Nicole set the letter aside and gathered herself. She needed to take a long breath before reading the words more carefully. Anne's letter forced her to contemplate questions for which she had no answers. Nicole felt the inner conflict—happiness for Anne and Thomas, for Charles and Judith and their coming marriages. But when was the wedding? Nicole quickly reread the letter. In truth, the double ceremony had already taken place. This in itself came as yet another shock. To learn of their shared joy after the events had taken place only intensified the emotional blow. Anne would be staying in the safe world of Charles's home and wealth with Thomas to love her and baby John. For a brief moment Nicole longed to be back there herself. But, no, she sighed, and to her own ears it sounded resigned. No. She couldn't go back. She'd left because it was not her place, not her home, not where she belonged.

But where was her place? Where was her intended

home? What was to be her life's course? What was she to do here in America? Should she declare her loyalty to this land? And what about Gordon—where did she stand with him? Was she right in requiring him to share her faith? He was clearly a good man for whom she had deep feelings. Was this not enough?

Nicole stared down at the letter in her hands. These pages she held formed a mirror. It was as if she were looking down at all her doubts and worries, all reflecting back at her with a clarity and intensity she could hardly bear. She needed to resolve these issues in her life. But how? She had prayed and studied the Scriptures, and what had she discovered?

She put the letter down beside the teacup she hadn't yet touched. Rising from the chair, she stepped over to the door, turning once to look back at the table and the letter. No, she couldn't think about it just then. It was too much. She needed . . .

She swung the door open and walked down the hall. Gordon was seated alone in the dining room. He stood slowly, looking tall and stalwart and alone. The light filtering in through the side windows was gray and cold, and rain beat steady against the glass. She could hear the wind rush across the roof and echo throughout the stone-walled chamber, a blustering sound that only added to her loneliness and bewilderment.

Gordon must have sensed her dilemma. "Is something wrong?" he asked.

"No, the letter . . . I expected to find Pastor Collins."

"He had to see to some matter." Gordon took a step toward her. "Was there news from England?"

"Yes, everything is . . . well, Anne is married."

"Your sister? My hearty felicitations." But there was no indication in either expression or voice of finding any pleasure in the news. "Nicole, we must speak."

"Gordon, please, I . . ." Her heart thudded within and she could not go on.

He squared his shoulders and spoke in a voice that didn't require much volume to command. "Yes, it must be now."

She nodded once and sank into a chair at the table. Now it was to be. And why not? She'd had weeks and weeks to decide. What could be gained in delaying the matter any longer? And yet her heart fluttered within her chest like a frantic bird in captivity.

Gordon returned to his seat. Now that the moment had come, he seemed unable to collect himself. He took several deep breaths. "My dear Nicole, you must be aware that more than mere obligation has compelled me to accompany you on these journeys."

She nodded. Not because of his words, but because she already knew what he was about to say. Just as with Anne's letter, Nicole somehow sensed the message even before he said it. She turned inwardly to God, crying, begging Him for an answer. A direction. A moment of calm and clarity.

"I have accepted these responsibilities out of my growing affection for you." Gordon spoke with the quiet forcefulness of one who had thought long and hard over his words. "I have sought to show you through my deeds just what sort of man you have encountered. A man whom you can trust to uphold your concerns as his own. A man who seeks nothing more than your joy and your trust. And, God willing, your love."

"God willing," she echoed in a whisper. *God, please speak to me. Tell me what I should do here, what I should say.*

"The longer we are together, the deeper my affections have become." Gordon reached across the table. "I have hoped for some sign from you, some beacon that, were I to pay suit, you would respond favorably. I have waited and hoped through many trials. But I can wait no longer.

The world is turning, Nicole. Times are harsh and pressing in from all sides."

"Gordon—"

"Please, I beg you, let me finish. You have not asked me to do so, but I should be willing to give up the sea. Even with the chance for advancement and a future, I would put my career aside. And willingly. Without hesitation or provision." Then he took her hand, held it with both of his, and said, "If only you will accept my suit and agree to become my wife."

There it was. The words she had dreamed of, yearned for. And dreaded. She clenched her eyes shut for a long moment and pleaded once more for God to make His will known to her.

When she opened her eyes, it was to find Gordon eyeing her with the bleak countenance of one who already knew he'd been denied. "Is it such a hard thing that I ask?" he said.

"No. No, it is not." In fact, it was so easy that to say anything but a wholehearted *yes* left her quaking with fear that she would be making a terrible mistake. She searched the silent chamber, the stone walls, the roof, the rain-spattered windows. And found nothing.

"You may as well speak it aloud," he said dismally, withdrawing his hands from hers. "I can see it already upon your face."

Nicole stared across the table. The anguish in her heart lay between them. "Why are you not able to believe with me?"

Of all that she might have said, this clearly was what he least expected.

"I beg your pardon?" said Gordon.

"*Believe!*" The word echoed back at her, its starkness shouting that perhaps she was trying to convince herself as well. "To share my life with you means you must share my faith in God! I have tried to make that clear to you. You speak of commitment and obligation. So do I. You say you have tried to show me who you are. That I have done too. And yet you have refused me, time and time again."

"Refused you?" His voice was incredulous.

"But you have! Every morning and evening, each time I invited you to join me in reading the Scriptures, in prayer. I *begged* you. And your constant response was no. How else can I answer you now?"

"My Nicole," Gordon began slowly, "I shall speak frankly. Strong woman that you are, I fail to see why you insist upon being so enamored with religion."

"I—you—"

"Wait, I beg you. I have no problem with the church, with faith, in its proper place. But all of life must be kept in reasonable balance. Wind and sail and tide and season, all must be brought into harmony. Then will the ship run taut and true and hold to its correct course."

"Impossible," she murmured. Not at his words but at the dilemma she faced. "It is impossible."

"On the contrary," he argued. "I speak with the reason of one who has survived troubles and storms that I doubt you could scarce imagine." Again he reached for her hand. "This I promise you, on the power of our love and the future I desire to give you. No captain can doubt the power of God. Yet this must be matched by a will tested and seasoned by the sea."

This time it was Nicole who withdrew her hand. She finally said, "I fear I have nothing more I can say to you."

"Indeed." Gordon rose from the table, his expression downcast. "Then I have no choice but to bid you a good day."

A good day? Her heart echoed the words with a pain so deep she clasped her hands to her breast.

Chapter 12

The harbor master conducted his business from a stone hut positioned at the wharf's most seaward point. A squadron of fourteen longboats had been drawn up alongside the hut, the oars laid out in proper military fashion to await their next call. The harbor wasn't particularly busy, as the blockade squadron was out to sea and the war delayed the onset of spring trading.

This much Gordon had picked up from tavern scuttlebutt over a glum lunch. His men had settled at another table, one closer to the door, leaving their captain well alone. Officers were granted unquestioned isolation at times, and never had Gordon needed it more than now. A black rage had swept over him, only to depart and leave him so miserable he had longed for the fury again just to keep him from drowning in despair. He'd tried to focus on the talk from other tables so as to avert his attention from the storm within.

The table across from him held a group of merchants up from New York, quaking in their boots over the prospect of being caught up in a battle. Things had been fairly quiet all winter. Yet there were signs of coming conflict, especially on the roads leading north. And word had it the Americans were preparing likewise. This meant the merchants had received top price for their goods. If only they now could return in safety to their homes.

Gordon left the inn and crossed the rocky beach toward the harbor master's quarters. His men continued to hold well back. Gordon hadn't spoken a dozen words to them since departing the hostel, only that they would be bunking on board the vessel. When one of the soldiers dared ask if Nicole would be joining them, Gordon had resisted the urge to raise his fists to the rain-drenched sky and rage at the futility of everything. His negative response prevented any further questions.

He knocked on the stout oak door of the hut. Hearing a call from within, he opened and said, "A good afternoon to you, Master," determinedly courteous in spite of his inner anguish.

Like most good harbor chiefs, this one was retired navy. His grizzled, weather-beaten features born of countless watches before the mast matched a voice that was the bark of one long used to hailing the topgallants. "Do I know you, sir?" he rasped out.

"No, but I hope and pray you know my vessel. Captain Gordon Goodwind at your service."

"Goodwind, Goodwind, where have I heard that name. . . ?" Bushy silver eyebrows shot up until they disappeared beneath the brow of his cap. "One moment, Captain."

He went to the open window, peered into the distance, and shouted, "Avast there, Tyler! I say, Tyler!"

A stocky youth came bounding across the rocky beach. "Aye, sir?"

"Run, do what I told you. Don't just stand there, lad! Hop to it!"

"He's here?"

"Just you do as I said, and be right smart about it!" The master slammed the window shut, then scrambled about his desk till he came up with a long-stemmed clay pipe. "Will you join me in a bowl, Captain?"

"Thank you, sir. But the pleasures of tobacco have thus far eluded me." Even while he stood there with the sounds and smells of the sea all around him, Gordon felt none of the anticipation that normally accompanied a new voyage. "If you'll excuse me, sir, we have just journeyed from the back of beyond. My men and I are quite exhausted and eager to get on board."

"Certainly. Won't keep you a moment." But the master refused to meet Gordon's eye as he spoke. Instead he searched the potbellied stove for tinder, then made a studied business of lighting his pipe. Through wreaths of smoke, he finally continued, "There's just the matter of some documents not left in my care."

"Forgive me, sir, but I fail to understand. We sold and off-loaded all our stock prior to heading inland."

"Yes, well, that is . . ." The master moved back to the window and looked with some consternation through the glass. "Here they come!" he cried. "Now we'll have it all out and done!"

But before the harbor master could reach the door, it flew open and Carter exclaimed, "Captain, a dozen or so redcoats with arms at the ready are headed this way!"

"Aye, and they'll sort you out right smart if you try anything!" the harbor master said, shoving his way outside. He waved frantically to the rapidly trotting soldiers. "This way, lads! This is them here!"

At a barked command from the lead officer, the troops split into two lines and flanked the stunned and confused men. Once the soldiers were in position, the officer ordered, "Hands off your weapons!"

Instantly Gordon realized what was afoot. He felt his mouth tighten with his gut. "You men there, do as the officer says."

The officer watched them obey Gordon with the steely-eyed mien of one ready for bloodshed. "All right, now drop your arms and step away!"

115

"Excuse me, sir," countered Gordon firmly, "but you haven't the right to do this."

"Are you Gordon Goodwind?"

"*Captain* Goodwind, yes. And who are you?"

"Lieutenant Driscoll. I fear you are captain no longer," he sneered.

"Of course," Gordon said with a calm born from one who had over the years learned to recognize the quiet before great storms. "You have commandeered my ship."

Gordon's matter-of-fact acceptance rattled the officer. "You knew?"

"Not until you arrived, sir. But it is evident, is it not?"

"You—" The officer and the harbor master exchanged glances. "You are not surprised?"

"Our nation is at war. It is only natural that—" A slight motion caught the corner of his eye. "You! Wilkins! Hold hard there!" Gordon shouted.

One of the other men moaned the protest. "But, sir! Our ship, she's—"

"Hold hard, I say!" Gordon turned back to the officer but directed his words to his men. "The king's official representative is the garrison commandant. If he has requisitioned our ship, there's naught we can do. Is that not the lay of the land, Lieutenant?"

"Indeed it is." The officer kept one eye on Gordon's sword hand as he reached into his pouch and extracted a bundle of papers. "Here are the proper documents, including your payment voucher."

Gordon took his time with inspection of the papers, knowing the longer he remained calm, the less risk there was of a violent exchange. Then his eye fell on the second sheet, and dumbfounded, he said, "You have press-ganged my men still on board the ship."

"The ship needed skilled hands to sail her," the officer responded impassively. He waved a hand at the rest of Gordon's men. "These too are to come with me."

"I am afraid not, sir." Gordon rolled up the documents and stowed them away in his tunic. "Your orders were to acquire the men upon the vessel. This you have done. These men are my hired hands, here on land, with no ship to be found."

"This is outrageous!" he sputtered.

"A strange choice of words, given the circumstances." Gordon turned to the harbor master. His back to the army officer, he revealed a trace of desperation. "Would you not say I have assessed the matter correctly, sir?"

Being former navy, Gordon assumed the harbor master was no doubt familiar with the horrors of press-ganging, where sweeps were made of many English ports, emptying taverns and inns of all able-bodied men between the ages of sixteen and forty-five. Regardless of their family situation or lack of knowledge of the sea, these unfortunates were chained and led on board ships with neither notice nor any way to contact their kin. They were forced belowdecks and held there until the vessel was well away from port and were kept in service until, if they survived, the war's end.

The harbor master squinted through his smoking pipe, inspected Gordon's features, then faced the officer and said, "I must stand with the captain here on this matter, sir."

"Nonsense! We have been ordered—"

"I heard the orders same as you. And Captain Goodwind has responded to the loss of his vessel as well as any officer I've ever known."

"You can't possibly suggest we leave these men here under his charge!"

"That's exactly what I suggest. There will be no trouble here, Lieutenant, so I bid you a good day." To Gordon, the harbor master said, "You won't be making trouble for me, now, will you?"

"What is there to be gained by such measures?"

"Nothing good at all, and much bad." Since the officer stayed standing where he was, the harbor master barked, "I said good day to you, sir!"

"I'll be having words with Colonel Grudge about this!" the officer huffed as he turned on a heel.

"No doubt you will."

The lieutenant stomped to the rear of the line. "Company, about face! Double file! Rapid march!"

After the redcoats had left, the harbor master said to Gordon, "I didn't have a thing to do with the loss of your ship, Captain."

"I am well aware of who is responsible," Gordon said, his gaze fastened on the backs of the retreating redcoats.

"You've met Colonel Grudge?"

"Once. And that was enough."

"Aye, I know what you mean." The harbor master tapped his pipe against the hut's corner post. "A word to the wise. Grudge was out there on your vessel for an hour and more, hunting about for something. Came back hot as a poker straight from the fire. Something about your having gold that was his by right."

"The gold is mine," said Gordon, "or rather the vessel's former owners. Fair payment for goods he purchased off my ship."

"Be that as it may, Grudge will be looking for a reason to lock you up. He was the one who ordered me to have the lieutenant down here, warning me you'd be causing all sorts of trouble. I'm thinking, now that's what he was hoping you'd do."

There was nothing more to be gained from standing here, so Gordon gave the harbor master a bow of military precision. "Sir, I thank you for your aid in regard to my men."

"Think nothing of it." He blew on the cold pipe, then stowed it in his pea coat. "Lost a vessel once in the last war. The conflict started when we was out to sea. We had no notice of the change, so headed into the docks at Calais calm as you please, where them Frenchies stole my boat and bound me and my men in chains. That was bad enough. Hate to think what it'd be like to lose a boat to my own side." The harbor master gave Gordon a sympathetic salute. "You handled it well, Captain. Good day."

Gordon turned to his men, who were watching him with blank amazement. He knew what they were thinking. That he had shown weakness for the first time anyone could remember. He had walked away from a fight, admitted defeat, and left the field with his tail tucked between his legs. He guessed they were within a hairsbreadth of revolt. He couldn't control this, nor could he alter their course. He signaled for them to follow and then onward he walked, not bothering to look back. Either they came or they didn't. The truth was, Gordon felt more defeated than ever in his entire life. And with no place to go, for they had taken his ship.

One point the harbor master had completely wrong. He'd said Gordon's ship had been stolen by his side. Whatever reservations he might've had about declaring for this new land were now gone. The British had lied and they had stolen. No longer could he remain on their side or even neutral. The American Revolution was his now.

Chapter 13

To Nicole's dismay, Pastor Collins did not return that afternoon or evening. Over a solitary dinner she overheard that one of the students had just lost a brother to the conflict, and the reverend had gone to console the family. The seminary and all the hostel guests were affected by the loss, for apparently everyone knew the family. The evening chapel was a muted, sorrowful time. That suited Nicole perfectly. She dabbed at the corners of her eyes as she continued to cry, this despite her best efforts to put behind her what had happened with Gordon. There was nothing to be done about it, she told herself over and over. Gordon had made his choice, and she hers. Her grief became mingled with that of her neighbors, until she felt as though they all wept for the same reason, for the same fallen and discouraging circumstances.

As before, her room was little more than a private cell and contained just enough space for the smallest of her trunks, a slat bed, a chair, and a candlestand. When she had closed the door on the night, Nicole stood with head bowed and fists clenched tight, determined not to let go and weep again for all that had been lost. Her home and perhaps destiny, her love—all gone before their time. Yes, *love* was the only word to describe her feelings for Gordon. She'd never seen it as clearly as she did right now,

standing in this little closet of a room, feeling lost and for-
lorn.

Deliberately Nicole moved about to prepare herself for
sleep. She blew out the candle. She then slipped into bed,
pulled up the blanket to her chin, and lay there with her
fists still tight across her chest. The darkness and the stone
walls echoed back her muffled sobs. All was lost. Everything. And she heard no voice from heaven.

———— ✿ ————

Gordon's progress away from the harbor was accompanied by heavy remorse. His men kept a careful distance
as they followed him back into the wind-lashed rain. The
cobblestones shone slick and turned dangerous in the day's
dying light. He stopped one person after another, asking
each in turn for the finest tavern in all of Boston. His motley band of men ended up on the seaward side of Beacon
Hill, in a place with a roaring fire, burnished pewter
plates, and bustling servants. Thankfully there was an open
table away from the door, in as private a corner as the
establishment offered. Gordon motioned his men to take
their seats.

The innkeeper came over, eyeing them with a war-
weary gaze. "We don't want no trouble in this place, good
sirs."

"Well, you'll be having none from us," Gordon
replied, too overcome from the day to take offense. "We
seek nothing more than a good repast and a quiet alcove."

"You men will find both here." Still appearing uneasy,
the innkeeper added, "There's a company of officers in the
next room."

"Your warning is well taken," said Gordon in a low
voice. "I assure you there's no need for alarm." He could
understand the man's concern. Weary, wet, and bearded,

he and his men were strained after two weeks of hard riding. "We'll have a round of your finest cider and whatever you're serving that's fresh and hot."

Nervously the innkeeper said, "Wartime prices being what they are, you'll naturally be wanting to pay in advance."

Gordon saw Carter begin to rise in offense. He nodded at the bosun to sit back down, then told the innkeeper, "Most certainly."

When the sovereigns were counted out, Gordon found there were but five left jingling in his deerskin pouch. He shoved the pouch back in his pocket and waited till the mugs of cider and bowls of fresh-baked bread were set down before them. Then he leaned in close to the little group and began straight in. "I'll say this as clearly as I know how. Our ship is gone, our mates are press-ganged, and we're betrayed. As far as I'm concerned, my own allegiance to Britain is over and done."

The bosun looked at him with raised eyebrows. "You're aiming to move to the other side?"

"That's right. My brothers are risking their lives for what they feel is their destiny and that of their families. For years I have been drawn by their arguments and their dreams. And now the last loyalty I've had to Britain has just been sundered. Mind you, I have no intention of bearing arms against my former countrymen. But there's bound to be other work I can perform for the American colonists."

Carter turned to the others in triumph. "Didn't I say the captain would never run from a fight? He was just regrouping, waiting to fight another day."

"No fighting, if I can help it," Gordon repeated.

But the bosun wasn't finished. "The sign of a wise commander, if ever I saw one." Carter turned back to him and said, "I'm your man, Captain."

"I can't hold any of you men to your oaths," Gordon

continued. "You're free to go as you will. This is my personal battle."

"The whole way back, we've been talking," a gunner's mate said with a rumbling voice. "That was good land going for the asking out there."

"Land we couldn't dream of owning back in the old country," another agreed.

It was a hard thing for Gordon to say, yet the option had to be laid out here and now. "You men could just go now," he said. "The horses are yours for the claiming. It's the least I can do, since there are no monies left for your back wages. If or when all this is over, I promise I'll do my best to see that the shipowners do you right. But for now, a horse and your liberty papers are all I can offer."

Following this were quick signs around the table, looks read by those who had together weathered storms and countless miles on windswept decks. Then the bosun answered, "We're with you one and all, Skipper. A fairer hand we've never seen. Just give us your word that when this is over you'll do what you can to help us get our own land."

"You have my solemn word," said Gordon, emotion making his voice sound strangled to his own ears. "And my earnest thanks as well."

"Begging your pardon, sir," the gunner's mate said, "but what will become of Miss Nicole?"

Gordon felt the cold, wet wind blow hard across his heart once more. "If only I knew the answer to that, I would walk from here a contented man."

Chapter 14

"If I am not imposing, Reverend, may I have a word with you?"

Pastor Collins lifted his head from the text he held in one hand, and with the other, he pulled off his round-rimmed reading glasses. He studied the young woman standing before him. Pale and timorous, she wasn't her usual confident self, but instead held a haunted darkness. He cleared his throat and nodded to her, waving his glasses toward the seat opposite his own.

"You could never be imposing." He smiled at his own poor choice of words. "No, you are always imposing, but as to a charge of being an imposition, that never, my dear."

Nicole seemed to find it hard to smile in response.

"Please, sit down. I can see that something is disturbing you deeply. If a listening ear will be of any help, I offer both."

Nicole didn't sit at ease. Her back stayed arched away from the chair's wooden back, and her hands twisted nervously in the folds of her gown.

The pastor laid his book to the side, placed his glasses on the small pine table at his elbow, and leaned slightly forward. "Have you received more bad news?"

Nicole shook her head. "No, nothing. Nothing more." The words brought no relief to her eyes.

"But you are worried, yes?"

Her eyes dropped, and for a moment she didn't speak. When she did raise her head once again, she looked directly into his eyes. "I carry worries of the heart."

He gave only a nod in reply and watched Nicole toy with the lace of her sleeve. The pastor reached for his glasses. "I'm not sure that I am the one to give counsel on such matters. Perhaps the spiritual heart. But the human heart . . ."

She looked up. "Perhaps . . . perhaps they are one and the same," Nicole offered.

He couldn't help but smile as he replied, "Yes, that may be true."

Nicole leaned back. "I came here to Massachusetts with quite different expectations," she began, then bit her lip. "You know I expected to take up residence at my uncle's estate. My estate, actually. He had given it to me, to administer the property for the good of those who needed its bounty. But now those plans, those dreams, are not to be realized. I don't know what I am to do, what plans I should make. Or can make. It's all so puzzling. And the war—I fear I will be hemmed in and unable even to return back to my home, whether south or north or to England. I feel trapped, helpless. Worse than that, I feel useless."

"And with reason, I believe," said Pastor Collins.

"I don't understand why God did not allow me to take up this good work as intended. It's not that it wasn't needed. In fact, it will be even more necessary for the surrounding communities in the days to come if this . . . this insanity of war continues." Nicole shook her head. "Why did He allow me to pursue this purpose if He deemed it to be the wrong course? Surely my uncle's estate would have benefited many."

"My dear child, you have asked some valid questions, but you must also bear in mind that God is not the only force active in our troubled world. Since the entrance of sin, God has granted permission—for a time only, mind you—for the evil one to also have claim to this earth on which we dwell."

"Of course," said Nicole. "I have not forgotten."

"So you see that it was not just *your* plan for good that was thwarted, but God's plan as well."

"You mean—?"

"I mean that your uncle Charles could have been quite in step with God's plan for the Harrow estate. You could have been in step with God's plan too in your seeking to carry out your uncle's intent. But the evil one—he seeks only to alter, to destroy, to engage all of the power at his disposal to keep God's plans from being fulfilled. He stops at nothing and uses anyone willing to be his tool."

Nicole's "I see" was barely a whisper.

"But one is not to despair over setbacks or inconveniences. God is not blind. Nor powerless. He has other ways, other means. Though the devil often appears to be the victor, he is not. Only momentarily at seeming advantage. But the tide will turn. God has other ways to accomplish His purposes. He has not been blindsided, of that you can be certain."

He leaned back in his chair and joined his hands over his ample girth. His eyes took on a sparkle that Nicole hadn't noticed before. "Quite frankly," he said, "I find it invigorating. Better than a game of chess. Satan moves. God checks. God moves. Satan counters. It sometimes looks like checkmate, but it never is. Not for the enemy of our soul. God always outplays him. Always."

"So you are saying—"

"*Wait*, my dear. Wait to see what God's next move might be."

"You're saying God always rectifies?"

"No," said the pastor, "I am not saying that. The evil one does destroy. Does cause much pain and suffering and loss. He does oppose and upset God's plans for God's people. But this does not need to defeat us. Because it does not defeat God. His overall plan for mankind—to take us from a troubled earth to a perfect heaven—that will be accomplished for all who trust His way. That is our hope. We mustn't let temporary setbacks in a temporary world cause us to retreat and fail to keep that hope alive."

Nicole wiped at her eyes. She asked Pastor Collins, "What then should be my next move?"

His eyes found the window as he shifted on the padded seat to rub two gnarled hands together slowly. "I wish—" he began, then started over—"no, it would be quite wrong of me to chart your course for you. That must come from God himself."

"You are saying—"

"I'm saying I do not have the direction you're seeking. You must find it for yourself. With God's help. I am not wise enough, nor perfect enough, to line the way out for you. God alone will reveal the way, and in His time." He leaned forward. "But there is more resting upon your mind and heart, yes?"

"After these weightier matters, affairs of the heart seem rather trivial," Nicole murmured.

"Well, I don't regard them as such. Not at all."

Nicole's cheeks flushed, and Pastor Collins watched her face intently. "It's . . . Captain Goodwind."

"A fine man."

"Yes. Yes, he is. But not a Christian in any but name, I fear."

Pastor Collins shifted position again, leaning back more heavily on the well-seasoned chair. "I expected as much," he said.

Nicole's head came up. "I cannot accept the suit of a man who does not share my faith," she told him, her tone forthright.

"You would welcome such were he of a different mind?"

"Oh yes." The words came quickly.

"Then I would suggest that prayer and patience are what's needed."

"But I have prayed—"

"And the patience?"

Nicole's smile was tremulous. "Perhaps the patience is lacking," she confessed.

"The hardest part."

"It does seem so," she agreed, sounding surprised at his understanding.

Pastor Collins retrieved his glasses and book. The lamp beside him flickered as a wisp of air current brightened the flame.

Nicole rose to her feet. "I do thank you for the wise counsel, both now and in the past. It seems that by now I should be able to untangle these complexities of faith on my own. But—"

"Never be afraid to seek counsel, my dear. We have been put here to be of help to one another. If anything this poor servant of God can say is of use in strengthening your faith, then I feel both deeply humbled and rewarded."

Nicole looked as though she would step forward and place a kiss on his bearded cheek. Instead she again expressed to him her thanks.

Just as she turned to go, he spoke once more. "Patience," he repeated. "God always has His answers ready and in plenty of time."

Chapter 15

A day's journey inland from Boston revealed every river crossing to be closely guarded by British soldiers. But then just before nightfall, Gordon and his men happened upon a fisherman who was only too willing to row them across in exchange for two of Gordon's remaining gold sovereigns. They waited till the dark of night, then crossed in two groups. Once on the other side they quickly set up camp and, exhausted, slept where they were. The next morning Gordon spent another sovereign on a farmhouse breakfast for everyone, consisting of eggs and fresh bread and dried fruit.

Downriver they found the American garrison encamped in and around Cambridge. Before entering the village, Gordon gathered all their weaponry except for the long knives, wrapped them in an oilskin bundle, and buried it near a huge elm tree. A hundred paces later they were hailed by an outer sentry. After searching them for weapons, the sentry allowed Gordon and the others to pass through. Neither their dress nor their purpose caused any great interest. Gordon had the distinct impression that a great number of men were straggling into Cambridge, their goal being to enlist in the American cause. What was left of Gordon's gold was spent on bread, cheese, and a jug of winter cider. With these packed away, they bivouacked beneath a sheltering maple.

The following day they made their way toward the village common. There was a certain unfamiliar quality to the army's main garrison, something Gordon noticed almost as soon as he set eyes on it. Yet he couldn't say exactly what it was. A few glances at his men told him they were equally confused. The soldiers they encountered looked weary and far less equipped than the British. But the garrison itself seemed in good spirits, however, with the music of fife and concertina and mouth harp rising from several groups. It was only after he'd stopped two soldiers and asked directions to the garrison headquarters that Gordon finally said, "I have it."

"Sir?" said Carter.

"The difference. Don't tell me you haven't noticed it."

"Aye, there's a feeling to this place I can't put my finger on," the bosun agreed.

"These are free men." Gordon waved a hand about the place. Every stretch of green was covered with motley tents and men. "Point out to me the officers."

His men turned and searched. Carter said, "They have to be here, sir."

"Of course they are. But there's none of the stiffness you'd expect within a British compound. You see, these are *free* men, none of them press-ganged and brought here against their will. They're here because they want to be here. They're fighting for a cause they believe in."

He watched his men try to wrap their minds around the utterly foreign concept. Most had come into the service as boys and done so because they had little choice in the matter. It was either through the merchant service, the navy, the army, an apprenticeship to someone born into wealth, or a guild. Gordon moved toward the redbrick building that was pointed out as the garrison headquarters.

"You men stay here while I get a glimpse of the lay of the land."

The stark contrast between the British and American attitudes was even more apparent inside the headquarters. Men came and went here in easy liberty. The officers held command, yet they didn't boast in their superiority. They ordered and the men obeyed, simple as that. A structured military system had definitely been put in place. And yet as Gordon stood in the anteroom and waited for someone to address him, he saw indications that here was something entirely different from anything he'd ever seen before. Finally, as an aide ushered him to a side office, the word came to him. These soldiers were *volunteers.*

"Captain Goodwind, do I have that correct?"

"You do. At your service, sir."

The officer didn't bother to rise or introduce himself. He indicated a chair across from his desk, using a leather-hilted dagger as a pointer. A blue longcoat with the stars of senior rank was tossed over a gun rack in the corner. "Have a seat, Captain. Now then, do I understand you and your men wish to join us in our cause?"

"That's correct, sir. I admit it may sound a bit unorthodox, but we wish to formally declare for the colonies."

"You mean the *former* colonies," the officer corrected sharply.

"Of course. Forgive me." Gordon glanced over to where the aide stood. Almost slouched, really, showing none of the deference Gordon would have expected. The man observed him with undisguised curiosity.

The officer inquired of Gordon, "You have military experience?"

"Of a sort. I was raised through the ranks of His Majesty's merchant navy."

"And now you intend to join with us. Interesting."

Gordon gave a brief overview of all that had happened. The man listened intently without attempting to hide his skepticism. When Gordon mentioned his family ties to the Virginia militia, the officer asked his aide, "Do we have anybody about here from that far south?"

"I believe Samuels is from Richmond, sir."

"See if you can locate him."

The conversation between Gordon and the officer turned to the inconsequential until the aide returned with a bearded dark-haired man who wore a tattered longcoat with a colonel's markings on it. The man took one look at Gordon and exclaimed, "Saints above, you could only be a Goodwind!"

"That's right, sir. Do you happen to know my brothers?"

"Aye, count both as friends." He pumped Gordon's hand. "Isaac Samuels, from Richmond."

"Gordon Goodwind. An honor, sir. What can you tell me of my family?"

"Your brothers are well, last I heard. Their families are growing. They tend towards daughters, the both of them. Eldest was born the same week as my middle boy, going on twelve now." A pause, then, "There's been some heavy battles down our way as of late."

"So I've been told."

He clapped Gordon on the shoulder. "Never you mind. If any will walk away sound in mind and limb from this mess, it's your two brothers." To the officer behind the desk he said, "If this man is cut from the same cloth as his kin, we're well served if he will join our cause."

"Well, that's good enough for me." For the first time, the officer stood from his chair and offered his hand to Gordon. "General Phillip Mitchell, Captain. Welcome to the ranks of the American Colonial Army."

"Nay, that won't do, not do at all." The bearded man clapped Gordon's shoulder a second time. "What the man means to say is, Welcome home."

"Your arrival couldn't have come at a better time, Captain." The officer signaled to his aide and said, "Go find that liaison fellow."

"Right away, sir."

General Mitchell turned back to Gordon and continued, "Our navy, such as it is, is scattered to the back of beyond. The ships are located at smaller ports from Maine down to the Chesapeake."

"Not that we don't have some good men and fine ships," Colonel Samuels added. "We've just laid keel to a new one by the name of *Constitution*. To be built from Georgia live oak, I'm told. A wood hard as old iron."

"Be that as it may, our problem is supplies," said the general. "The British are choking us off, most especially by sea. We don't have enough clothes, food, powder, lead, artillery, even men."

"But there's good news!" an excited Samuels interjected. "At long last."

"Aye, that there is," said Mitchell. "We've just received word that the French have declared for America."

"That could make all the difference," Samuels said, and Gordon nodded agreement.

"What I need to know from you, Captain, is how familiar you are with the coastline."

"Quite well, sir. I've sailed vessels about these waters for a dozen years now."

The two American officers exchanged a silent communication. Mitchell said, "Very well, then. I understand a French fleet is making its way down the coast and carrying much-needed supplies. I want to assign you a boat. It's not much for a man of your talents, no more than a fishing vessel that's used to hugging the coast."

Gordon was quite certain it would be rather primitive. "No doubt it will do us fine, General," he said.

"The boat will serve the purpose we have in mind and little else. We must connect with this fleet before they encounter the British blockade. You will be sent north with instructions to guide the French away from the Boston harbor and lead them up the coast to Newbury. Do you know it?"

"I confess not, sir."

"No matter. It's a hamlet, nothing more."

"But it won't be known to the British."

"Precisely. We'll have runners at the ready, and as soon as you signal, we'll send up a brigade to cart the supplies down to us here." He scribbled on a square of parchment, dusted the page, then handed it to Gordon. "The officer in charge of our efforts is one Captain Langford. But there's every chance you won't see him at all. He and his ships are all stationed along the New Hampshire coast, hoping to locate the Frenchies before they ever draw near." He inspected Gordon with a keen eye. "You and a few others will be our final line of warning before the Frenchies sail right into British hands."

"I won't let you down, sir."

"We'll all be glad of that." At a knock on his door, the general said, "Come in!"

The general's aide reentered, escorting a warrior. At least that was Gordon's immediate impression.

"Captain Goodwind, may I introduce you to Henri Robichaud. He is French by way of Louisiana, and will act as your translator and go-between." Gordon reached out to shake his hand and found a grip as hard as iron.

Chapter 16

The vessel was just as Gordon had envisioned, a floating hulk with rags for sails. He halted his sailors' protest by saying, "Never you mind, lads. We'll do our stint, help guide the newcomers to shore and safety, and be off to better things."

The Frenchman, Henri Robichaud, was certainly an enigma. The way he twisted his frame so as to look back over his shoulder, his features set in scorn, left Gordon wondering if the man hadn't spent a lifetime perfecting the manner. Hate seemed to smolder in the dusky eyes. Not just fury at Gordon, but at life in all its bitter forms. "So . . . the British officer finds the boat not to his liking? Too much sweat and hard work for the gentleman? No place for him to set his cup of tea?" he flung out in his French-accented words.

"Hold hard, men," Gordon commanded, not needing to look over his shoulder to know how his men were responding. "I am the same as you, Robichaud. A man seeking a country."

"You're not like me at all, *Captain*. We have nothing in common, you and I. You have heard perhaps of the Acadians?"

Gordon chose to turn away without response. The shoreline was too exposed for his liking, the British side barely out of rifle range. There was the faintest glimmer of daylight left, enough to reveal the mist rising from the waters and drifting shoreward. The wind had died, though the night remained overcast and far too cold for late April. The other side of the river was quiet. Gordon had the sense of unseen eyes holding steady upon him. He looked back to find that Robichaud had moved silently forward and was alongside him now.

"The Acadians, Captain. They are my people. Theirs is my story. It is a tragic tale, one I am sure will not be to your liking. A tale of treachery and woe, of how the British swept up an entire people from their homes and flung them to every corner of the globe."

"I know the Acadian saga," said Gordon. "I even know someone who has endured as you have."

"There are any number of the poor wastrels wandering about." Robichaud's hand continued to knead the sword's hilt as if desperately hungry to pull the blade free. "All because of you and your kind, English Captain."

Was the man actually seeking to call him out? Here and now, after they had been given a direct command by garrison headquarters? Gordon studied the tightly drawn face opposite him and realized there were no words that would reverse this situation. Easing his feet farther apart, he readied himself to unleash a first hard swing of his own weapon.

Robichaud no doubt caught the subtle shift, another sign of an experienced swordsman. He gave Gordon another of his taunting scowls, then wheeled about and stomped out onto the boat. "Are we to remain standing here upon the shore all night?"

Gordon could scarcely believe the encounter had ended without a fight. "All right, men! Heave hard! Let's get this lady afloat."

Robichaud didn't offer to assist them, which was not altogether a bad thing. It had reached the point where even his own men looked ready to do the man in.

The boat slid easily from the bank and rested steady in the thigh-deep water. Like many such fishing vessels never meant to leave sight of land, her draw was shallow and her keel but an extension of the rudder. Gordon ordered six men to places at the oars, while Carter and two others rigged the lateen sail and sent it aloft.

All the while Robichaud sat at the very peak of the bow, looking out across the fog-draped river, the long dagger taken out now and resting in his hands. The oars were well greased and moved quietly up and down within their locks. Once the sail was set to catch what little breath of wind there was, the only sound was that of the oars dripping and sighing softly as the men put their backs into the work.

Then, to Gordon's astonishment, he heard the unmistakable sound of a blade being drawn along a whetstone. In the silent air the grinding noise rang out as exaggerated and harsh. Gordon breathed, "For the sake of us all, Robichaud, cease with that racket!"

There was a subdued hiss in reply, but the noise halted.

The mist rose about them in billowing waves until Gordon could no longer see the way ahead even while standing on the center stanchion, using the mast to balance himself. He was about to order the slightest of his men to climb the mast and see if a light could be spotted, but decided first to whisper to Robichaud, "You are certain of our course?"

"Of course I am!" The man's rough voice sounded loud as a foghorn. "Don't tell me the British are frightened by a bit of night mist."

Gordon was thinking about having the man either silenced or tossed overboard when out of the thickening fog there arose apparitions from his worst nightmares. Three vessels, all of them filled to the brim with soldiers armed with muskets, all aimed straight at their chests.

British soldiers. British muskets. Aimed at them.

"Avast there!" The officer's cry was triumphant as if a victory were already theirs. "Keep your hands up high or face a broadside!"

"Hold fast!" Gordon shouted to his men. To the opposing officer he called, "We surrender."

"Well, well, if it isn't the darling Captain Goodwind and his band of merry men." The same officer who earlier had confronted Gordon at the harbor now stood at the bow of a longboat. "Colonel Grudge will be delighted to know he finally has you within his grasp. You men there! Lift your hands higher or we'll bury you right here in the river!"

Two of the longboats pulled up to either side of Gordon's vessel, which soon swarmed with marines brandishing pikes and sabers. As their mates in the longboats watched down the barrels of muskets, the marines lashed Gordon's arms behind his back, then did the same to his men. The officer clambered aboard then, and Gordon protested, "I am a British officer, sir. You have accepted my surrender. There is no need for these bonds."

"You are a spy and a traitor, sir." A torch was lit, and it seemed to Gordon that the officer's features contorted in angry glee. "I shall soon delight in seeing you dance a merry tune from the end of a rope."

Gordon watched as the officer turned and handed Henri Robichaud a hefty sack. "Fifty sovereigns, as we agreed. You can do more for us?"

Robichaud slipped the pouch into his pocket. "I will deliver both news and men into your hands, so long as you pay me in gold."

"Excellent. I shall have one of the boats row you ashore."

"No, it is better that I swim, in case there are any spying." Robichaud moved to the gunnel. "Give me three minutes, then fire a fusillade into the night."

"Very well. You have my gratitude and my government's."

Robichaud gave no sign he had even heard the officer's thanks. Instead he offered Gordon's silent rage another sneer. "You are wondering how I could do such a thing, yes? I have starved, Captain. That is something you can never understand. I made a new home in the south, only to lose that as well. I have almost died more times than I can count. And I have learned that money has no loyalty, nor country." He leaned closer to Gordon and added softly, "These British will also pay, but in my own time."

As he draped his legs over the boat's side, he said, "I shall go back to the Americans and say how I barely escaped from this Captain Goodwind, who proved to be nothing more than a turncoat. I shall say that no doubt he is now back with his own kind, laughing and drinking with the other rich officers, making jest over how blind and trusting and foolish the colonial soldiers were."

Then Robichaud slipped into the mist-clad waters and was gone.

Chapter 17

Nicole came from the seminary kitchens where she'd been giving a hand to the elderly cook. She hadn't found much to do to make herself feel useful, but at least she could pare the shriveled turnips or sort through the potatoes from the root cellar.

She certainly didn't enjoy the task. She looked at her stained hands with a measure of despair. They were no longer the soft hands of a lady. But Nicole had given up feeling like the lady of her recent memory. In fact, it was becoming increasingly difficult for her even to recall what had occupied her days while at Uncle Charles's mansion in England.

Still, what troubled her now was not the stains on her fingers. It was the fact that she had heard nothing—nothing in many days—about Captain Goodwind.

She'd spent the first several days in anticipation of hearing some word from him, then later, at the least, of him. But no word had come. Surely he hadn't gone off to sea without even a good-bye. . . .

The very thought left her feeling bereft and deserted. She had no place to call home. Her trunks full of her personal belongings were not at her disposal. She was forced to cover her dress with a borrowed laborer's apron. It would not have been so hard had she some assurance that this was to be for only a season, but Nicole had no way to free herself from her present dilemma. The future looked bleak. Was she to spend the rest of her days trapped within a seminary, peeling half-wasted vegetables? Quite a different life than what she'd envisioned, that of being in charge of a large and magnificent estate. Now she wasn't even in charge of her daily existence.

Never had Nicole longed so intensely for family. If only she could seek the counsel of her parents, whether Henri and Louise or Andrew and Catherine. If only she could pour out her broken heart to Anne. But the prospect of seeing any of them again was off in a very distant future. To make matters worse, her last link with all she'd known and depended on was gone with the passing from her life of Gordon Goodwind, leaving her alone, frustrated, and forsaken.

I guess he was not the man I thought him to be, her sorrowful heart grieved. There was no place to go for solace; everywhere she turned there were seminarians or servants busy with various chores. Her own room, with its walls of stone, felt too small, dark and confined to offer a place of refuge. How she longed for her cliffside retreat in Georgetown. She hastened forward along the quay, lifting her face heavenward and wondering whether God was still there, still listening when she called out to Him.

The horrid dream of the night before came back to haunt her. It had been of a vacant dark face. At first the figure was masked, hidden in misty shadows, then long, tendriled swamp moss. The eyes came sharply into focus—dark, steely, and menacing. And taunting her, even as they drew her forward. She seemed hypnotized. For it was against her will that she'd moved forward, until the eyes were all she could see before her. They danced with laughter, then flashed anger so intensely she shivered. Suddenly the eyes turned blood red, oozing forth some vile substance that began swallowing her up in a quagmire.

She had awakened with a cry, her hand pressed against her mouth until her lips hurt. Though the room was chilly, she felt the sweat dampening her body. With a whimper she clung to her one meager blanket, pulling it tightly about her, seeking some kind of protection against the terror.

It was Jean again. She knew the eyes all too well. After being free of nightmares of him for so many years, she was at a loss now as to why he'd returned to haunt her dreams once again. Anger took hold of her. She wished he were actually there so she might rail against him, fling her fury in his face as he had done to her.

But he was just an apparition. Even so, it all had left her unsettled. In the light of day it wasn't hard to understand that she had no cause to fear a dream. But in the dark desperate hours, he was all too real.

Her only defense was to sort through this while the midday sun blazed within a summer sky. There had to be a reason for the recurring nightmares, some way she could fight against them and win. Was it because she had come to suspect that the man she'd fallen in love with was another like Jean Dupree? Was Gordon just a more refined, more sophisticated version, of Jean—an arrogant and self-seeking man? When might the dark eyes of Jean become the eyes that Gordon had once turned upon her? Would they haunt her just as surely?

She needed to think. In the brightness of day she needed to pray. To work it through so that her nights could be peaceful again.

Nicole had ventured farther along the harbor than she intended, yet still hadn't found a desirable secluded spot. She cast her eyes around to be sure she was within shouting range of the seminary gardens should the need arise, then turned inland to look for a place where she might sit down.

A grove of hardwoods stood beyond the last house on

the lane she walked. The tangled shrubbery around the outer rim made access a challenge, but in her determined state, she lifted her skirts above her ankles and threaded her way through. Briars caught at her heavy stockings, threatening to tear them further. It was a problem she wished to avoid, for she was down to her last pair, this one already bearing much mending. She picked her way more carefully.

Once beyond the outer briars, the foliage thinned. Thankful, she dropped her skirt back to the tips of her dusty shoes and looked around for a likely spot. A sharp cough brought her head upright, and she prepared to take flight.

She was relieved to see Pastor Collins, eyes wide with surprise as he peered at her over spectacles perched precariously on the tip of his nose.

Nicole's hand had flown to her throat. It still fluttered there, trembling from the scare. "You frightened me almost to death!" she told him with a shaky laugh. She didn't say so, but she had half expected to stare into those haunting dark eyes of her nightmare.

"My apologies," begged the pastor, "but I was not expecting any company."

"I—I did not know anyone was here," Nicole said. "I was but seeking a quiet retreat to do some thinking and praying."

"The chapel would not suffice?"

"I needed some air, something—." She motioned with her arm. "It seems I am in great need to sort through some—" she groped lamely for words, "some inner searching."

He smiled, then patted the fallen tree that served as his bench. "Well, since we have interrupted one another, why don't you come sit down? Perhaps we can do our searching together."

Nicole still trembled as she accepted the proffered seat.

"Is this your first time to the grove?" he asked, and she felt he was trying to put her at ease.

"Yes," she admitted. "I usually stay much closer to the buildings."

"And so you should. It isn't safe for a young woman such as yourself to roam too far afield." There was no scolding in the words but more of a concerned warning. "But should you decide to come again, there is a path, halfway around the copse to our right. Not totally clear of brambles anymore, though still much more conducive to walking than the way you came."

Nicole nodded in silence.

"Tell me, what has driven you from the scullery on such a fine day?"

Nicole swallowed and dipped her head. "I'm afraid that my faith still is not what it should be," she said frankly.

"And what leads you to this conclusion?"

"I have been having terrible nightmares of late."

"So it is you who's been crying out in the dark hours."

Nicole was alarmed. "Have I been disturbing—?"

"Only the laundry lass in the next room. She spoke of it to me."

"I'm so sorry."

"You needn't let it upset you. She seemed not to be troubled by it— only concerned. But she didn't know from whence the cries had come."

Nicole was relieved that at least her secret had not become a subject of gossip at the seminary.

"Nightmares, you say. I would think the days in which we live would merit nightmares for all of us."

Nicole picked some burrs from the hem of her apron. "It's not just that I am having nightmares; it's the *kind* of nightmares."

He waited for her to go on.

"There was once this man," Nicole began slowly. She took a deep breath, deciding to bare her soul. "He was

Acadian. I thought at one time that I loved him. No, that is wrong. I did love him. Fiercely. But it was all wrong. He couldn't come to terms with what the British had done to us. Not like my father. Jean was never able to forgive. Which turned him bitter and angry. So angry that he vowed revenge. He frightened even me. He became consumed with getting even. I had to end the—the courtship."

"But you love him still?"

"No, no. I'm quite sure I am over the infatuation. It is not that which haunts my dreams."

"Then what?"

"I do not know. That is what disturbs me. All I see are his eyes. His eyes always full of hate and evil, always seeking to draw me in. To destroy me."

"Hatred. Bitterness. Revenge. They seek to destroy and too often they accomplish their goal."

"I know that. But I am a follower of Christ. There is no room in my life—my heart—for such evils. I cannot understand why now, after these years of walking with my Lord, I should be subject to such passions once again. Why must they haunt me?"

"You bear no malice toward the British?"

The question caught her totally off guard, but she was quick to respond. "None."

"Not even toward the young British captain?"

"Well, that . . . that certainly isn't because he is British," responded Nicole, her cheeks flushed.

"What is it, then?" the pastor asked.

She'd been caught in her own trap, exposing an anger she would have denied if questioned outright. "I'm puzzled," she stammered. "He declared his love for me and then he left, without so much as a good-bye or a trace of where he was going."

"Puzzled? And angry?"

Nicole could not deny it. "Perhaps. A little. I thought,

you see, that we could at least remain friends."

"But friendship was not what the young man sought."

"You know I could offer nothing more. We spoke of this. He refused to accept my faith."

"Your faith. Not his faith."

"Well, it would have been his faith, of course. Faith is personal. Not something handed from one to another."

"But you wanted to hand it to him, did you not?"

"I merely wished to lead him. To introduce him to my Lord. Is that wrong?"

"My dear, my entire life has been lived to introduce others to our Savior. Nothing could be more right."

"Then what did I do wrong?"

"I have not said you've done anything wrong, my child. I am simply saying that the road we travel toward faith can take us through different valleys and around different twists and turns. What brings one soul to his knees might be a stumbling stone to another. We cannot expect another to travel our personal pathway. In our past conversations, you have spoken of your own struggles. Adversity brought you to our Lord. Another's faith might come because of unsolicited joy. God's holy goodness might burst out suddenly, exposing all the glories of a life walked in harmony. That might be enough to make one fall to his knees in deep gratitude. Paul walked the Damascus Road. It was the light that felled him, the voice that drew him. For James and John, Peter the fisherman, it was the simple invitation to 'Come, follow me.' So to some the invitation might come as a clarion call, to another a soft whisper."

"But surely hard times and coming to the end of one's own resources must soften a soul," Nicole dared respond.

"Soften? Not always. Some souls respond to the rains of adversity by becoming pliable, while others are hardened into unworkable clay. Some grow in faith, are strengthened, honed, harmonized, while others turn bitter, angry—like your former friend Jean. Either we shape our adversity into something of beauty, or it shapes us into something vile."

They sat in silence. Above their heads a crow cawed and was answered by a second crow from farther down the grove. A squirrel chattered angrily. Apparently the crows had invaded his private territory.

Nicole picked at another burr. "What am I to do?" she asked. "I do not want to be hardened by the heaviness of the load I carry. How does one make sure that the treading, the beating down, is used for good?"

The kind old gentleman shook his head. "I have no answers for you, my child. That is not a simple question, and has been asked before in many a heart. You're a young woman now, no longer a child that needs to be led by the hand in relation to your faith. You have sought, and found, many answers already. Only God can help you to find the rest. I am your friend, here for you whenever you need a listening ear. I cannot tell you the answers to life's complexities. But with God's help and through prayer and the Scriptures, you will find the way. His divine wisdom is as available to you as it is to me."

It was a troubling yet glorious thought, and Nicole found herself reaching for it, claiming it as a sacred promise. She had free access to a holy, all-powerful, loving Father.

"It is ever our challenge to draw closer to the Master's heart. To search for His way through life's maze. With each step that we take with Him, our faith deepens, our steps become more certain. Take your dreams, your fears, your struggles, and use them for stepping stones to Him, my child. Let every issue of life be a means of bringing you closer to the Shepherd."

Nicole fought against tears, but not ones of sorrow. Once again her soul felt comforted, strengthened. She was ready to move on.

Pastor Collins stood. "Come, my dear," he said. "I

shall show you the path so your skirts might not catch any more burrs and brambles." He led the way to an opening at the edge of the tree line. Nicole noticed that his step was rather slow and lumbering. She wondered for a moment how many more years he might have left to serve. And also, how they ever would get along without him.

Chapter 18

The only cheer in Gordon's endless first day of imprisonment came with the evening meal. He was being held separate from the others, confined in what resembled a cowshed, with rotting branches and tarred paper for a roof. But at dusk he was permitted to join the line and take up a bowl of gruel and hardtack with the other prisoners. Most were wastrels and ne'er-do-wells, and it galled him terribly to be counted among them. What hurt even worse, what truly ravaged his mind and spirit, was to see his good, fine men standing in line with these others, reduced to prison and chains by his own miscalculations and poor leadership.

Yet even here the men made a place for him, sidling about until Carter was able to whisper unseen by the hovering guards, "Word has it, we're to be shipped off day after tomorrow."

"What?"

"Press-ganged. Two ships from the blockade are headed into port. A bout of scurvy has laid waste their ranks." Carter's ankle chains clinked as he shuffled forward in the meal line. "They're in dire need of men who know one end of a rope from the other."

Though being press-ganged was not good news, Gordon felt his heart lift that his men would not hang with him. "You don't know what it means to hear this."

"Aye, sir, we thought you'd be pleased." But Carter's grimy features showed no joy. "If only we could do something about your situation."

"No hope there, I fear." Gordon worked to put a brave face on it all. "But knowing you lads won't be climbing the scaffold as well, that will send me off content."

As the sun fell below the parapet the day's dankness worked its way into the prisoners' bones. Gordon followed the example of the more experienced captives and ate his gruel slowly, letting the warmth of each spoonful work against the discomfort of his wet clothes. As the air chilled, the wet earth on which they sat in their prison clothes produced the effect of steam emanating from their shoulders and shirt sleeves. Faint tendrils rose up from the bodies of his men, as though all hope were being drawn from them and dissipating into a gray and uncaring twilight.

Through the deepening gloom there came something new. Gordon turned and searched before his mind registered precisely what it was he was seeing.

The man in the rector's collar was barely more than a youth, or so it seemed against the backdrop of chains and mud and miserable prisoners. His boots and the hem of his longcoat were caked with the prison yard's red mud. But in the flickering torchlight he seemed to carry a special atmosphere with him. The prisoners responded with but a few words. But they seemed to sit a bit straighter after he passed. When the pastor came upon their little group, he greeted them with, "You men are new here, are you not? I don't recall seeing any of these faces before."

"That's right, Reverend," said Gordon, answering for them all. Then he said quickly, "Might I ask where you hail from?"

"New Haven, originally."

"No, sir. I meant, which church?"

"Ah. Well, actually, I am still attending seminary." When he smiled he appeared even younger. "If my professors are to be believed, I may be there still when I am old and gray."

Gordon rose to his feet but addressed his words to the soldier standing guard nearby. "I would beg a word with the pastor in my cell."

"But you have not finished your meal," the reverend pointed out.

Gordon handed his bowl to Carter. The barrel-chested man clearly understood what was afoot, for his eyes gleamed as they met Gordon's gaze. When the soldier waved them on, Gordon said, "Might I speak with you privately, sir?"

"Of course."

Evidently the pastor was expecting the penitent lament of a man facing the gallows, because his first words after entering the place where Gordon was held were, "Do you know our Lord and Savior, sir?"

"Not as well as I should." Gordon remained quiet while the guard refastened his ankle chains to the shackles embedded in the wall. After he left, Gordon lowered his voice and said, "I must get word to someone staying at the hostel by the harbor seminary."

The young seminarian looked stricken. "That is not possible."

"I beg of you, sir! Lives are at stake here."

"May I ask your name?"

"Gordon Goodwind."

"Ah. Certainly. I have heard of you." The pastor glanced behind him at the barred doorway, then whispered, "Sir, I have given my solemn word to speak of nothing here save the gospel."

"Then I cannot, I shall not, ask you to break your word. But if you see it within your reach to simply mention to a certain Miss Nicole Harrow—"

"The Lady Harrow? I saw her just this morning."

"She is well?"

"Most certainly. She . . ." The young man bit down hard on his lip. "Sir, I beg you. My oath."

"Yes. Of course. Only if you were to perhaps mention that we have met, you would receive my undying gratitude."

The young man retreated toward the doorway as he said, "Sir, I urge you to think anew of your Savior and *His* undying gift."

Chapter 19

Around midnight Nicole got up from her rumpled bed. She couldn't sleep with her mind so full of questions. She pulled on her robe, lit a candle, and sat down at the little table. Just above her head, a simple cross hung on the stone wall. She found herself talking in her mind to God, asking why solutions were so hard to find. The answers seemed further from her now than when living in England. She sought with all her might to do His will. How could He remain silent for so long, and in the midst of such a troubling time?

She yearned for her sister's companionship. Her thoughtful, wise counsel. Anne's most remarkable ability was how she could genuinely live the moment with another. During the times they had spent together, Nicole had the impression of speaking to another side of her own self. She desperately needed this gift now.

Nicole drew out a quill and sheet of paper from her trunk. Fortunately the table's inkstand was almost full. Even as she began writing, she knew full well she would not be sending the letter, at least not any time soon. According to what she'd heard in the dining hall, mail on its way to England was notoriously slow, if it arrived at all. Yet instead of feeling frustrated, Nicole found herself invigorated by the thought that, while writing to her sister, the words might come in a way that would help bring understanding for herself, perhaps revealing truth.

So it was that she began her missive with one of the hardest questions of her entire life. What would have happened if she and Anne had not been exchanged as infants? What if their assumption had been wrong, the surmise that made it possible for Nicole to find a certain reason in all the pain and hardship that had followed: What if Anne had indeed been strong enough to survive the long journey to Louisiana? Did that mean that everything Nicole endured in her stead was only the result of happenstance, of life's uncaring hand?

She paused there, marveling at how there was no anguish in her soul at such considerations. She felt as if the night blanketed her with a comforting closeness, as if it sheltered her heart so that her mind might explore forbidden pathways. This was the clearest sign she could have received from an otherwise silent God—at least seemingly so. Maybe she was in fact not alone. She dipped the pen into the inkstand and continued.

Nicole imagined how it might have been for Anne if she had traveled her road and, later on, helped to build their home in the Cajun country. In truth, she knew and so wrote, Anne would never have been a fighter. Her spirit didn't contain Nicole's restless impatience, her challenge to circumstance. She may have lived through the road's travails, yes, but emotionally she would not have thrived. Wilted and weak, she would have silently moved through a life too severe for her gentle spirit. The constant struggle to adapt and survive would have overwhelmed her. The internal battles, which had only sharpened Nicole's desire to grow and travel and see and experience, would most likely have proved too much for Anne.

Nicole spent a long moment cleaning the quill's nib, pressing it again and again on the ink-stained scrap. She knew what the next question was to be, and she didn't flinch from it. She was merely gathering herself. She dipped the quill, took a long breath, and asked of the night: If she had remained in Nova Scotia, what would have happened to her?

The answer came easier here, perhaps because the search for truth was well under way now. The letter had become a journey into life's imponderable questions. The answer was, she would very likely have fought against Andrew and the poverty that resulted from his and Catherine's choices. Another dip of the pen, another long breath. And she would have hated Anne. For this family she had never met, and probably never would, had robbed her of the more prosperous way of life accorded Andrew Harrow, a military officer. It would not have mattered that this wasn't the truth. In her dark and sheltered corner of a war-torn world, Nicole saw herself with utter clarity. The restless younger Nicole would have *made* it the truth. Why? Because it would have made her parents her adversaries, opening the door to the conflict her impatient spirit demanded.

She used the hem of her robe to clear her eyes and then returned to her writing, now at a furious pace, desperate to keep up with her tumbling thoughts. She also would have loathed how Andrew and Catherine's choices had caused them to become ostracized by the military and by polite society. Even though she might have agreed with their position, still she would have fought them over the result.

As the night wore on, Nicole came to realize that Henri Robichaud's staunch and unbending faith was precisely what she had required. Catherine and Andrew might not have been able to withstand her strong will and rebellion.

The night's hardest confession was that in the end she might well have come to oppose her father's faith. She could have blamed God, and fought Him as well.

If the switch had never been made, perhaps Anne might have survived physically, yet despaired emotionally. Nicole, on the other hand, would have thrived in Nova Scotia in one sense, but she may well have lost herself spiritually. And thus lost everything.

This confession stripped her to the bone. Nicole stared at the bottom of the final page and saw written there the words her hand only in part had made. God did indeed work all things for the good.

The candle flickered once, then dimmed. She watched it burn down to a final nothingness and disappear into a tiny glowing ember. Yet the night's comforting closeness only drew nearer, holding her still in its embrace. Nicole rose from her chair, took off her robe, and climbed back into bed. She stared up at the unseen ceiling and wrote more words there with her heart. What was the purpose behind all she was experiencing now? What were the lessons to be learned?

The night's final question she whispered, the sound as a faint echo to her heart's cry. "Gordon, Gordon, where have you gone?"

The next morning Nicole ate a solitary breakfast with only her Bible for company. Chapel wasn't for another half hour, and her room's tiny confines seemed far too restrictive just then. She could feel eyes upon her from the other tables and could guess what they were thinking. A young woman on her own, mysterious and silent, and so the rumors swirled. That she was a titled lady, an heiress and a daughter to a Nova Scotian pastor. No, a daughter of an Acadian family. Nicole sighed hard enough to push away the thoughts and concentrated harder on the words in front of her.

"Ah, there you are." Pastor Collins stepped through the doorway and hurried over to where she sat. "How are you, my dear?"

"I'm well, thank you." She did not say more because she could see that a deep strain creased his forehead. "Is something troubling you?"

"Perhaps I might ask you to come this way."

"Of course." She followed him from the dining hall and waited till they were on their way back to his office before she said, "I hope the seminary hasn't lost another friend to this horrible war."

To her dismay, Pastor Collins responded only by opening his office door and saying, "Please come in."

A young man shot up from his seat when they entered. Nervously he twisted a wide-brimmed hat in his hands, one often used by New England clergy. Pastor Collins said, "May I introduce the soon-to-be Reverend Peters. This is our dear Lady Harrow."

Nicole started to ask that he use her given name, when she saw the two of them watched her with shared expressions of concern. Then the strength went out of her legs.

Thankfully, Pastor Collins was alert and able to grip her elbow. "Here, my dear, please seat yourself here."

She allowed herself to be guided into a chair, then forced the words through a throat that had clenched tight with terror. "It's Gordon, isn't it?"

Pastor Collins turned and nodded to the young seminarian, who swallowed and said, "I have been granted license to minister to the prisoners within the British garrison's stockade."

"Stockade? Gordon? But that's—"

"Allow the young man to continue, my dear," Pastor Collins cautioned gently.

"The entire garrison is speaking of nothing else. Which is why I feel I can convey this news without breaking my word." A shaky breath, then, "Gordon Goodwind was captured in the act of sailing an American vessel out of harbor. He is to be hanged as a turncoat."

Nicole could only stare at him. But clearly he understood the unspoken question in her gaze, for he added, "In three days' time. On the same day, his men are to be given the lash and then press-ganged."

She bowed her head over her knees. She felt Pastor Collins's hand come to rest on her shoulder, but the sensation receded into the far distance. As in the previous night, despite the tumult and the feeling of her heart being squeezed in her chest, she felt a peace come over her. And so she waited. She had no answers. She had no direction. Nicole leaned over with her forehead planted on her hands, her eyes tightly shut, and she permitted her mind's frantic whirl of emotion to recede as well. For once, she refused to give in to her restless energy. For once, she would remain still within her own helplessness. She would accept her blindness, her lack of answers, and wait for the divine hand to point the way. Nicole stayed as she was, scarcely breathing.

When she rose up, she found both men looking at her expectantly. She said quietly, "I must ask where you and your colleagues stand in this conflict against the colonials."

"The proper term for those opposing the British, my dear, is *American*," Pastor Collins responded. "It is a tragedy we see all too often just now. Families have become split over the question of where their loyalties lie. So within these walls, we hold to one allegiance and one only. To our Lord and Savior. That is how we maintain peace. That is how we shall survive."

Nicole nodded slowly, taking in both this and the implication that some within these walls were for the other side. "I must go to the Americans," she said calmly.

"My dear," the pastor objected, "that is a most

perilous thought. You could find yourself in danger, right alongside the good captain."

"Nonetheless, that is what I must do. And today." She then stood and addressed the young seminarian. "Can you help me?"

Chapter 20

The track through the marshland had turned boggy from the week's constant rain. In parts the trail disappeared completely, merging with the surrounding swamp and vanishing beneath rain-speckled water. The four horses stumbled and snorted and whinnied in protest, their flanks steaming. Overhead the branches appeared gray in the faint first light of dawn. Nicole could barely make out the pastor and the second man buried in the folds of their dark greatcoats. Their tricornered hats became funnels that poured a continual stream of water onto their horses.

The man had a knife scar that almost divided his nose in two. His eyes were gray and half hidden below eyebrows that seemed determined to grow until they joined up with his unkempt beard. He hadn't spoken at all. The young seminarian had offered no name, introducing him only as a trusted ally.

At a signal Nicole missed entirely, the trio halted. The seminarian watched as the other man unstrapped two long canvas-covered bundles from the fourth horse and said to Nicole, "This is as far as I dare go."

"I cannot thank you enough, Reverend Peters," she said.

The young man obviously took no pleasure in Nicole's gratitude. "You are certain of your course, ma'am?"

In reply, she slipped down from her horse, walked over, and patted his boot. "If you see Gordon—"

"Please, my lady, I beg you."

"Yes. All right. Of course."

The man led the horses into a thicket so dense that after five paces Nicole couldn't see them anymore. Swiftly he returned and hefted the bundles, holding them snug under each arm. He then glanced at Nicole, turned, and began hiking into the murky dawn. Nicole said to the young pastor, "Thank you again."

"Go with God, my lady."

"I hope so," Nicole murmured, the words meant for herself alone. "I do most certainly hope and pray that He is with me."

The man led her along what could hardly be called a trail. To her eye it seemed to be nothing more than another clump of grass, a tiny glimpse of soggy earth rising from the water, a stunted tree. Yet the water level never came above her ankles, while to either side she saw fish jumping and water birds diving for their food. Her boots kept getting caught and held by the muck, and each step required her to jerk hard to pull her foot free. The man never looked back a single time to make sure she was keeping up but slogged onto the riverbank, where he dumped his bundles into a boat that Nicole hadn't noticed until she was standing over it. He dragged the camouflage branches off the skiff, pushed it out into the water, and held it steady for Nicole as she climbed aboard. All without speaking a word.

The oarlocks were caked with old grease, the oars wrapped with an oily netting so as to give off no sound. He grunted softly as he plied them in a steady beat, pulling away and into the stream. Soon the bank was lost behind a curtain of driving rain. The swiftly flowing water was gray as the sky, as the day, as her heart. What was she doing? What did she expect to accomplish? Nicole bowed her head and watched the rivulet of water gush off the edge of her hood. *O Lord God in heaven, bless me this day, bless my actions. Please guide me. Show me what is intended here. Reveal to me the purpose behind this risk. Give me strength and courage. Amen, O Lord. Amen.*

The shore appeared out of the rain and the gathering daylight. Clearly the man had made this journey many times before, as he maneuvered the boat into a tiny creek that suddenly revealed itself among the undergrowth. He continued to pull them forward until the oars were touching either bank, then he tied the leader to an overhanging branch, stowed the oars, and stepped into thigh-deep water. He guided the skiff over to the bank and held it firm for Nicole to step out. Afterward he hoisted his two bundles and headed away.

Only then did Nicole realize he was leaving her alone. "Wait!" she called after him.

Reluctantly the man turned about.

"Which way to the Americans?" she asked.

He used a bundle to point toward the northwest.

"When do you return to the other side?"

The man's entire face worked, as though it required much labor to extract the single word, "Dusk."

With that, he turned and was gone.

The walk began in sheets of rain, although it seemed to her she'd scarcely gotten started along the trail before the rain tapered off. Had she not been outside in it, she would not have believed such a transformation could occur so swiftly. All she felt was the lightest puff of breeze upon her cheek, just enough to toss a few blustery droplets off her hood and onto her face. Yet up above the clouds seemed to be plucked asunder as a higher wind ripped away the heavy cover and revealed a morning of splendor.

By the time she caught sight of the church's spires, the day was already so warm she had dropped her hood and opened the front of her cloak. The surrounding fields and orchards had awakened with a flourish. The birds sounded so loud to her ears she suspected they also were enthralled by the sudden change of weather.

The trail broadened and became a brick-paved road. This was something she'd always loved about villages in England, how they kept their towns so much neater by paving the main roads. Boston had such, of course. But Boston was a very imposing place, with many large houses and tall, fortified walls and structures. Boston was a city striving for grandness. This was a village. *Cambridge*, she read on a shop front—a lovely, English-sounding name.

The farther she walked through the village, the more she was enchanted. Even in the midst of war, Boston held to a grandeur that reminded her of London's self-importance. Cambridge, on the other hand, held tastes of everything she had loved about England. And this was the perfect day to explore it, with the air sparkling from its recent scrubbing and the first hints of springtime green tracing new edges around the trees and shrubs. The houses were either split-timbered in the Elizabethan style or more staid and stalwart, dressed in stone and red brick. High-pitched roofs opened to dormer windows glinting merry and bejeweled, chimneys gave off woodsmoke, and the smells of morning meals lingered in the air. She heard a child's laughter and smiled in reply. Truly this would be a very nice place to call home.

"Well, hello there, my darling missy!" A rakish man wearing a saber and double pistols across his chest doffed his hat and bowed so low the peacock feather in his brim scraped the earth. His mates chuckled at the theatrics, ogling her. "How's about a kiss to greet the day?"

Not even this rudeness could ruin the day's fine spirit. Despite their lack of uniforms, their stance and watchful gazes caused Nicole to approach and inquire, "Are you soldiers?"

"That we are, missy. That we are." The man settled the hat back on his head, cocking it and grinning at her. Even with the dirt and the hour, the man presented a dashing look. "Unless you make it a point not to kiss soldiers. Then we'll just have to be whatever it is that delights you."

"I require a guide, sir. But I shall bestow my affection upon none save the lifelong companion chosen for me by my Lord."

The man seemed taken aback by her poise and her response. "Then he is a lucky man."

"Will you guide me?"

"That depends upon where you are headed."

"I seek a word with the American military commander."

The man was no longer smiling. "You have business at garrison headquarters?"

"I do."

"I make it a point not to get within cannon range of the officers. But for you, my fine lass, I will make an exception."

The man dispersed his companions with a single motion of his hand. As he and Nicole walked toward the center of town, the soldier asked her, "From where do you come?"

"That, sir, is a difficult question to answer." After a

pause, she said, "Acadia to begin with, then by sea and overland to Louisiana. From there to Nova Scotia, and then to England. Then back to Nova Scotia and now here."

"A lady who carries mystery in every word." He pointed to a brick structure alongside a village green. The square was nearly lost beneath a neatly cordoned company of tents, weapons, flags, campfires, and men. "There's the commandant's quarters. What is your business there, if I might be so bold?"

"My true love—" Nicole said and had to stop. For saying it had brought a burning rush of emotion to her throat, and her eyes filled with tears. She quickly blinked them away and said, "Forgive me, good sir."

"It's been a long time since a pretty lass called me *good*. Tell me, has your beau run off for the army?"

She wondered if this man could perhaps help her. "May I trust you, sir?"

"Ah, now, if only you would," he replied, but the smile was no longer rakish.

"My beau, as you call him, is being held at the British stockade as a traitor. I have come seeking answers. And help."

The news pushed him back a step. "He was caught working for our boys—for us Americans?"

"That I do not know. But I think so, yes." She struggled to form the words. "He is due to hang the day after tomorrow."

"That is hard news. What is his name?"

"Captain Gordon Goodwind."

"And yours?"

The question silenced her. What *was* her name? Who was she? Again tears threatened to force their way out. Questions and more questions.

The man moved in close and removed his hat. "It's not an easy world, is it, miss?"

Nicole gave a tiny shudder in agreement. "No, not easy at all."

"There's something about you that makes me miss all the things I've lost since, well, since all this started." The man looked down to where his fingers fumbled with his hat's brim. "It's a strange thing to say about a man facing the noose, but I'd count myself lucky to stand in his boots." He then looked her in the eye and said, "You can trust me with your name, miss."

"Very well," she whispered. "I am the Viscountess Lady Nicole Harrow."

By the time the soldier returned to escort her inside, there were faces in every window and more watching her from the front portico. "This way, your ladyship."

"Please, I decry such titles. I used it only because the matter is so pressing." She did her best to ignore all the eyes fixed on her. "Forgive me, sir, but I do not even know your name."

"John Jackson, most recently of Philadelphia. And many's the day I wish I never left. But today is not one of them." He cocked his head and with a solemn look on his face said, "There's something about you that makes me wish I was a far better man."

"I sense there is more goodness about you than you give yourself credit for, Mr. Jackson."

He led her up the stairs, through the throng of officers, and into one of the front rooms. "This is the lady herself, General."

"Mitchell's the name," the man barked, not rising from his desk. "So you're a duchess, do I have that right?"

"Viscountess, sir, but please—"

"And what might you have about your person to confirm this claim of yours?"

Nicole fumbled with the clasp of her cloak. Jackson was there to help her. Underneath she wore a day frock of emerald green, mud spattered and damp despite the cloak's covering. Even so, the officer's eyes widened at the evident grandeur of her gown. Nicole opened the leather carryall she had hung over her shoulder and extracted an oilskin pouch. From this she withdrew the oft-folded document. "Perhaps this will help to answer your questions, sir."

The general eyed the document for a long moment before murmuring, "You carry a treaty signed by our Continental Congress. Why, I see here the signature of General Washington himself."

Only when the whispered exclamations were heard did the general realize his door was still open. "I say there, get back to your duties! Shut that door, will you? What did you say your name was?"

"Jackson, sir. Sergeant Jackson."

The general glanced down at the treaty again. "Harrow. Harrow. I know that name."

"My uncle wished to help establish hostels for those made widows or homeless by the war."

"Of course. I remember now. Sir Charles Harrow spoke up for us in the British Parliament."

"That is correct."

"You were there?"

"Yes, I had the honor."

"Wish I'd seen it myself." He stood and gestured to the chair. "You must excuse me, ma'am. To have a beautiful young lady arrive on my doorstep and declare herself to be both a viscountess and the champion of a man I thought a turncoat, well—"

Nicole cried, "You know Gordon?"

"I've met him, yes. Know him, no. Not at all. My first impression was that of a good man, an officer we could trust with a difficult and vital mission. Then the Frenchie we had assigned him as liaison returned to say that the man was nothing more than a spy, sent here to study our ranks and gather information for the coming British attack."

"Please, sir, you must believe me. I do not know precisely what has happened, or even why Gordon came to you. But one thing I can say with all the certainty this heart can muster. If Captain Goodwind declared himself for you and your cause, he can be trusted with your life and the lives of all your men."

The general appeared uncertain, even anxious. He said to Jackson, "Have my aide come in."

The young officer must have been standing just outside the door, for he appeared at lightning speed. "You wanted me, sir?"

"What's the name of that Frenchie we sent off with the English captain?"

"Robichaud, sir. Henri Robichaud."

Nicole only managed to aim her collapse so that she fell onto a nearby chair and not the floor.

"A trustworthy chap, wouldn't you say?" Then he must have noticed Nicole's state. "What on earth's the matter?"

"I . . . that is . . ." She felt the room swirling about her. "Forgive me."

"You've gone white as a ghost." From a side table the general poured her a glass of water. He brought it over and said, "Here, now."

"Thank you," she managed through stiff lips. Her mind raced frantically as she sipped.

"Do you know this Frenchie fellow?" the general asked.

"I . . . I am not certain. What was his name again, please?"

"Henri Robichaud," the aide offered, eyeing her

carefully. "He's a good man, sir. Hates the British with a passion. Fine a fighter as they come."

It could not be her father. It wasn't possible. Yet her mind couldn't escape the horror-stricken question that followed. What if it was? What possibly could have happened that might persuade her father to leave Louisiana and join the battle? Was her information false and had the British attacked the bayou country? What of her family?

Nicole realized the general was watching her. She handed back the glass and forced herself to present a calm façade. "Might I have a word with this—this French gentleman?"

The general turned to his aide, who responded, "He's off to the north, sir. You sent him yourself. To await the arrival of the French troops."

"Ah, yes, so I did." He turned back to Nicole. "You say you know this Robichaud?"

"No, perhaps the name only sounded . . ." She let her words trail off. It just could not be!

"Right, then." The general returned to his desk. "Much as I hate to see a good man swing, there is little we can do to rescue your officer gentleman. We are at war, and things are only going to heat up further once the spring season takes hold." He picked up a silver letter knife and jabbed idly at his leather portfolio. "Don't suppose you could give us any idea of the state of the British army."

Focusing on the general and his words proved to be a difficult task. Finally Nicole answered, "I'm sorry, sir, but all I can tell you for certain is that Boston is swarming with troops."

"That's no help at all, I'm afraid."

"Begging the general's pardon," Sergeant Jackson piped in. "Perhaps I could travel across with the lady here and have a look around." He glanced over. "That is, if you'll be returning to Boston."

"At dusk," Nicole confirmed. She had a thousand

questions. But they would have to wait. She had no choice but to force these new worries to the back of her mind. Gordon's life was what mattered at the moment.

"I know your sort," the general snapped at Jackson. "Your lot wouldn't volunteer for guard duty for General Washington himself."

"I suppose that's true enough, sir," said John Jackson slowly. "All I can say is, I've had myself a change of heart."

Nicole rose to her feet and said, "It would only be natural for a titled woman to arrive with a servant." She looked at Jackson. "I would be honored to have you accompany me, Sergeant Jackson."

Chapter 21

The day was spent in feverish activity. Within the first hour, Nicole was certain she had made the proper choice in agreeing to work with Sergeant John Jackson.

The officers were scornful in their dismissal of Jackson, speaking with him only because General Mitchell had ordered them to do so. They asked him a series of specific questions they needed answered—about horses, artillery, supplies, troop placement, signs of movement. But they clearly expected nothing from the man, not even that he would return. John Jackson glanced at Nicole from time to time during these interviews but did nothing to defend himself. Instead he seemed to draw strength of purpose from the mission—even from her. He endured the officers' contempt and said little.

Afterward Nicole insisted they acquire for him proper clothes as befitting the attendant of a titled lady. Walking the streets of Cambridge together, John Jackson was time and again greeted by his fellow soldiers with ribald familiarity. And the fact that he walked near a lovely young woman was evidently nothing unusual.

Here again John Jackson made no attempt to hide himself or defend his past. He endured their comments with a stoic grimace.

However, when she'd located a gentleman's clothier,

Nicole found it difficult to draw Jackson inside. "What is the matter?" she asked him.

"I dare not go in there, ma'am."

"And why not?"

"Begging your pardon, ma'am. But if I'm to act the part, I need to be starting now."

"Yes, very well. But come along inside."

"I'd best stay out here."

"How are we to determine the sizes if you remain outside?" Nicole pushed the door open and was welcomed by a sharp little chime. "Come along. There is hardly time for us to waste out here talking."

But as soon as Jackson stepped inside with her, Nicole understood. A young woman wearing the starched frilly apron and matching dust cap of a shop mistress gave an angry stare as she dropped into a sullen curtsy. "Good day, madame," the woman said.

"Good day. I have need of some clothes for my servant."

"Your servant, is it?" she repeated, her glare directed at John Jackson. "Your servant indeed."

A man's voice came from the back room, saying, "That will do, Matilda." A gray-haired shopkeeper appeared through the rear curtain. "Go and help with the sorting. Clothes, did you say, madame?"

"Yes, an entire ensemble," said Nicole, enduring a final furious glance from the young woman before she departed. "Which must all be ready in four hours."

The older man halted in the process of taking down a bolt of broadcloth. "I beg your pardon?"

"Four hours," Nicole confirmed. "Longcoat, frilled shirt, vest, breeches, stockings. Silver buttons on vest and coat and breeches."

"Silver buttons," the man repeated numbly. He glanced at the rear of the shop as there came an angry mutter. But he stiffened his shoulders and said, "Madame does of course realize there is a war on."

"I will pay handsomely," Nicole said and took out a small bag from under the folds of her dress. She untied the drawstring and spilled sovereigns into her hand. "You must be on time, sir. I hope that is quite clear."

Next they entered a boot shop farther along the lane. Here Nicole insisted on paying extra for a pair of buckled shoes on display to be refitted for Jackson's smaller feet, and done while they waited. It was only as they sat in the front room and listened to the shoemaker mutter and snip and hammer that the worries began to return. Hearing the name of Henri Robichaud spoken by the general was a hammer blow to her chest and returned each time she recalled the moment. But there was no time for such concerns. Not now. Nicole pushed away the anxiety as best she could, looked up at the grandfather clock standing in the shop's corner, and said to Jackson, "I do so hope we have time enough for you to have a proper bath, haircut, and shave."

Jackson protested, "Is that all necessary?"

"Most certainly." She cut off further comments by inquiring, "What does your family do back in Philadelphia, Jackson?"

He cleared his throat before answering, "My father is a minister."

"Indeed."

Jackson's expression was desolate. "You remind me of my sister. She was the one who held to our parents' chosen course."

"And you?"

"More like the wolf in sheep's clothing."

"I admire your honesty, Sergeant. Most men would try to mask what you have chosen to reveal."

A flicker of something new entered Jackson's eyes. "You'll excuse me for asking, but you are a believer?"

"I am."

He nodded. "I thought as much. Something in the way you hold yourself reminds me of everything I left behind."

Perhaps this was the answer, Nicole reflected. To meet this and every other encounter with faith. "None of us have moved so far from the Lord that we cannot return."

He searched her face. "You are certain of this, ma'am?"

"With every part of my being," Nicole replied. "I am convinced of this truth. As I am that your good parents would approve of how you and I have met this day."

Chapter 22

Nicole's sense of the rightness of joining forces and traveling with John Jackson was only strengthened on their journey to Boston as they left Cambridge with the westering sun. His strength of character and upbringing gradually became more and more evident.

The boatman scowled when Jackson came into view, but the sergeant met this with a steely-eyed frown that left the boatman silent. The two men held the boat for Nicole, then stowed two bundles of clothing and clambered aboard.

They sat and waited there till the night had fully gathered. The boatman then poled them from the creek, fitted the oars into their locks, and put his back into the crossing.

But he had scarcely dipped the oars a half-dozen times when Jackson issued a sharp hiss.

Instantly the oarsman held the oars in deep, bringing the skiff to an abrupt halt. He searched the dark, as did Nicole. She saw nothing, and given the oarsman's grunt, he didn't either. But when he slid into his backward position and began to draw out the oars, John Jackson reached over and gripped his arm without stopping his search of the water.

At the oarsman's protest, Jackson turned and gave the

man what Nicole could only describe as a sergeant's eye. So commanding was Jackson's expression that the other man immediately fell silent. They sat there, the fast current drawing them ever farther downriver. Finally Jackson lifted one hand and pointed. Nicole strained hard, but still she saw nothing.

Then there came the sound. Softer than the splash of a small fish. It would have been missed entirely had not all her senses been so tightly fixed in that direction. A swift glint of metal on metal. An even softer hiss in response. Then nothing.

But this was enough to have the oarsman backing them toward the American shore. They pulled into a draw created by two overhanging trees. Again they waited.

Overhead the clouds floated like dark islands in a silver-flecked sea. One of the clouds moved aside, and a rising quarter moon emerged. Instantly the river's tableau altered from empty black reaches to a trio of longboats. In each bow stood a man holding a musket. Oars dipped and pulled upriver as the hunters sought their quarry. But the moon was their enemy as well, and with its arrival orders were softly murmured. The boats were piloted about and aimed for the English side.

The three remained as they were for a long time still, the oarsman watching John Jackson now as much as the water. Only when Nicole's companion gave the signal did the oarsman pull them out into the swift-running river.

After they had arrived back at the seminary, Nicole paced the front chamber, impatient now for the next step. Thankfully Jackson didn't tarry, although he did reenter the hall with shamefaced chagrin. "I look like a regular fancy man," he told her.

"You look nothing of the sort," replied Nicole. It was a good thing Pastor Collins chose that moment to join them. "Please, sir, a moment of your time. Does my new manservant appear proper and fitting to call upon the garrison commandant's residence?"

The old man caught the undercurrent in Nicole's tone, so he gave John Jackson a careful inspection. Jackson looked even taller now, standing as he did in his knee breeches and tricornered hat and high-backed shoes. His dark stockings were drawn up tight, the frills of his shirt spilled from the top of his vest, and the buttons of his longcoat and vest and those at the knees of his breeches glinted in the light. Pastor Collins declared, "He looks every inch the proper gentleman butler."

"There, you see? Now tell me once more what you are to do."

"First I go to the commandant's private residence," Jackson began. "I am to ask for the chief manservant and present him with your card."

"And what do you say?"

"Compliments of the Viscountess Lady Nicole Harrow, and might she pay a visit upon the general's wife on the morrow."

"Yes, and then?"

"I am to inquire at the stables near the waterfront where your wagons and goods are stowed. I am to bring back the large trunk with the three leather straps and the iron lock. But I still say I should carry it myself."

"Nonsense. No proper lady's chief servant would be seen in such an endeavor. You shall find a pair of urchins and promise them a silver penny each. Now off with you." Jackson went over to the front door and reached for the sword that hung from the door strap. Nicole protested, "Must you go out armed?"

"This is a city at war," Pastor Collins reminded her. "He would look odd otherwise."

John Jackson strapped on his saber, whose well-worn hilt reminded Nicole of the risk they were taking. He reached for the door, then spun around and said gravely, "I won't let you down, my lady."

"I believe you," she said, feeling both exhilarated and full of anxiety.

Again he hesitated. Twice he started to speak, but when he did it was only to say, "I will do my best to earn the trust you have placed in me." Then he was gone.

She offered a fervent prayer heavenward and turned from the door to find Pastor Collins staring at her, a serious look on his face. Though it cost her dearly, she had no choice but to ask, "Would you have me leave?"

"Finding accommodations in this town is nigh on impossible," the pastor said, his tone indicating he had been considering this very thing. "Can you give me your word that you will not endanger us or our work here?"

Nicole took a deep breath and said, "No, good sir. In all honesty, I cannot."

He nodded slowly. "Then I must spend this night in prayer."

Chapter 23

The night wasn't nearly as dank as the previous one, and the day's warmth meant Gordon could air out his clothes and bedding. Now, as he lay on his blanket and rushes, he could gaze upward and see stars through the decaying roof. As the moon rose, it cast a silver mantilla through the barred window and door. Gordon felt as though the day was not altogether against him, a strange sensation for someone in ankle chains and fettered to a ring set on the cell's back wall. Yet he had a most remarkable sense of not being alone. He lay and drifted gradually away, and whispered to the stars and the night, "Nicole."

Then he heard the sound, quickly choked off.

He came up on one elbow and whispered urgently, "Who goes there?"

When there was no reply, Gordon wondered if fatigue had played a trick on his ears, that perhaps the sound hadn't been human at all, but rather a faint mewling from some distant creature.

Soon it came again, and this time he recognized it instantly. No man who had heard the sound would ever forget it. There always was one just before a battle, usually a youngster who was shipping out and facing naked steel for the very first time. Standing at his gun because there was no safer place aboard ship, with the adversary bearing down under full sail and nowhere to run. The young man—or, most likely, boy—would peer out across the sea and catch the reflection of sunlight off cannon and musket and saber. If the wind was right, he would smell the heated pitch of the smoky battle to come. He would catch a whiff of sulfur and saltpeter mixed in the gunpowder, which was being dragged up from the holds by the powder monkeys. He would hear the shouts from the enemy officers, who ordered their men to take no quarter, show no mercy. At that moment, from his place on the quarterdeck, Gordon would often hear the whimper of terror. The youngster usually wasn't aware he had even made the sound.

"Avast there," Gordon said in a low voice, repeating words he'd said countless times before. "Steady as she goes, sailor."

"Oh . . . sir," the broken young voice came through a crack in his side wall. "They are to hang me in two days."

"Nothing to be gained by wailing now, soldier. Did you do the deed you are accused of?"

"I was hungry, sir. Our supplies had not arrived, and I had not eaten since the morning before. The leather bag was there upon the table. How was I to know it belonged to an officer's wife?"

A terrible thing, justice in the forces. Particularly when at war. Gordon had said it often enough when faced with having to mete out punishments. But he had never endured the hanging of one of his own. And to have it happen to one so young. "Tragic," he murmured.

The word was enough to break the young man down entirely. "I'll never see my home again," he choked out.

Gordon moved back so that he leaned against the wall. He searched his mind for some comfort to offer. "Where is home for you, then?"

"S-Somerset. By the sea."

"I know it well. Your family are farming folk?"

"Aye, sir. Freeholders."

"Sheep?"

"And a few cows. My mam makes the finest butter in the county."

"Tell me about your home, lad." Gordon listened as the young man spun bittersweet tales of green pastures he would never see again and a family he had never missed so much as now. In his heart of hearts, Gordon felt an emptiness that was worse than anything he'd ever known before. His own coming demise he could handle. He knew he would climb those rickety gallows stairs and stand looking out over the gathered company, watch the hangman's sack come down over his face, and not flinch. But here and now, as he sat and listened to this young man, he felt bereft. Not for himself, but for what he could not offer this poor soul.

Gordon heard himself make comforting sounds, yet in truth he was struck by the realization of just how hollow was his own reserve of strength. At this point of direst need, his good right arm meant less than nothing. He was a leader unarmed.

The young man talked for hours, until finally his voice grew softer and softer and he slept. But Gordon was far from sleep himself. He sat there smitten by his utter lack of answers and any truth that was meaningful in this crisis.

The moonlight rose to where it pierced through the roof's largest hole. It fell upon his chains, as if even the night were intent on showing just how feeble his arguments were, how wrongheaded he had been in his final conversation with Nicole. She had been right all along.

Gordon slid around so that he knelt in the mud. The chains clinked together as he leaned over his knees and clenched both hands and eyes. It was too late to tell his beloved. But at least he could speak with God.

Chapter 24

Nicole spent the morning in whatever activities came to mind, so long as they kept her in public view. Her intention was for word to filter back to the garrison commandant's wife of a new lady in town. She knew from her experiences in London that there were few acceptable places for ladies with social standing to gather. Theirs was a tightly circumscribed world where they would not be forced to look too closely at the harsher aspects of life.

She had instructed John Jackson to ask about venues where the highborn ladies met together—the finest millinery, the proper tearoom. Her first stop was the Boston branch of Charles's bank, where she presented her papers and obtained a sizeable sum, paying an outrageous wartime premium for coin. She then went shopping and bought items she didn't need, allowing the money to slip through her fingers like water. She ordered hot chocolate merely because it was the most expensive item listed on the tearoom's menu, and, because of her nervousness, almost choked on the syrupy liquid. She sent John Jackson on a variety of errands, all of them issued in the manner of one who had ordered servants about all her life. She used her title at every occasion, and let it be known wherever possible that she was the niece of one of the richest men in England.

Her worst moment came while having lunch that day, just as the waiter set down her plate. She was chatting gaily with some ladies at the next table, agreeing with them that the war was a horrid nuisance, and the sooner the colonists were taught their place in the world, the better. Then a glint of light caused her to look up and see herself in the mirrors that lined one of the walls. She saw a lovely young lady with her chin held high, the face held in a mask of false smiles and empty words. But what captured Nicole's attention were the eyes. They held a look of desperation, of a lost and frightened child.

"I beg your pardon, ma'am."

Startled, Nicole looked around in surprise. John Jackson stood at respectful attention by her side. "Oh, excuse me . . ." She caught herself before she could be seen apologizing to a servant. "Where on earth have you been for so long?"

"Forgive me, my lady, but it's been hard to make progress on any front."

"Don't bother with excuses." There was something about the way Jackson held himself, or perhaps it was a new glimmer in his eyes, that caused her own heart rate to surge. "You have found what I sought?"

"It's hard to say, ma'am." He dropped his voice. "I fear they will not even discuss the matter unless they can see the weight of more coin."

"What?" This genuinely shocked her, for she had already that morning loaned the man thirty gold sovereigns, which was more money that most commoners would see in a year.

"It's the war, my lady. Everything costs more. Including what you wished me to obtain."

"Oh, my word, such prices!" the lady at the next table exclaimed. "Forgive me for overhearing, Lady Harrow. But the cost of things these days is out of sight. Why, just the other morning, I—"

"Yes, thank you." Nicole studied the man before her, hardly more than a stranger. She had no reason to trust him. And he gave off a certain tension that suggested the same thought might be going through his own mind. Could he be intending to take whatever more money he could receive and then vanish?

Nicole reached within her mantle and withdrew two leather sacks. A third she took from the little purse. "You will have to pay the gentleman by the door as you leave. I have nothing more."

Whatever John Jackson had expected, it was not this. His respectfully servile demeanor slipped away and he stared round-eyed at the weighty sacks she now held out to him. "My lady!"

"Go now." She pressed the pouches into his hands. "And hurry."

After Jackson had left, the woman seated at the neighboring table said, "My, but you are fortunate to have a servant you can trust with a king's ransom!"

"And so handsome," her neighbor's companion added. "In these awful times, how did you manage to keep him at your side?"

"Oh, he is most loyal," said Nicole weakly, wondering if she had not just made the most foolish decision.

Chapter 25

Nicole lingered a long while over a final cup of tea. In truth, there was nowhere else she could think of to go. Either the commandant's wife had heard of her expeditions, or she had not. Either John Jackson would return with progress, or he would not. She could not gather her strength to play the terrible charade any longer.

She sat and watched the folks strolling by outside the tearoom's front window and decided she could not at this point concern herself over questions of her future. She wasn't doing this in hopes of marrying Gordon. She had prayed, she had revealed her heartfelt concerns to him, she had received no answer, and so nothing had changed. Yet she must act to save this good man. It was that simple. Gordon Goodwind had done everything in his power to help her, and it had cost him his ship and many of his men. She had no course but to do likewise in his hour of most desperate need.

Then began the signs that her efforts were bearing fruit. First a soldier in the sparkling dress uniform of royal household cavalry stomped up the tearoom stairs, inquired of the gentleman at the door, then walked over to stop directly in front of Nicole's table and bow deeply. "Do I have the pleasure of addressing the Viscountess Lady Harrow?"

"That is correct, sir."

The soldier now saluted smartly. "My lady, the General Sir Gerald and Lady Weakes request the pleasure of your company this evening for a banquet in honor of the birthday of His Royal Highness, the Prince of Wales."

"Yes, I see." She pretended to consider this. "At what hour?"

"Seven of the clock, if it pleases my lady."

"Please convey my sincere gratitude to Lord and Lady Weakes. I accept their invitation with pleasure, sir."

The man gave another bow so precise it might have been formed with measuring rod and plumb line. "Very good, my lady."

Scarcely had the soldier departed than John Jackson appeared at the door. A single glance at his expression was enough to lift her from her chair. The waiter scurried over to pull back the table, but she was already moving across the floor to Jackson. "What have you found?" she whispered.

Jackson glanced quickly around the room and then said for everyone within range, "The shopkeeper has but one left, my lady. And the price he wants is ferocious."

"You will pay him."

"But, my lady—"

"Must I take care of this myself?" she said loudly.

"Perhaps it would be wise if you had a look, my lady. The price, well . . ."

"Oh, all right. Show me the way, then."

The gentleman was ready by the door. His bow was less grand than the soldier's, though far deeper. "It has been an honor to serve you, my lady. Please do come again."

John Jackson led her down the cobblestone lane, away from the finery atop Beacon Hill, and into the back alleys leading to North Point. They turned into a narrow, odorous passageway, where John Jackson finally halted and reached into his pocket. He handed over two of the leather sacks, saying, "One proved enough, ma'am."

"Never mind that."

Jackson glanced at her face, then shoved the sacks back in his longcoat. "It shouldn't be long now."

"Long for what?"

He tensed. "Quiet now. Not a word."

She heard the shuffle of footsteps, then the distant clank of chains and the murmur of exhausted men. Jackson pressed her back into the shadows and plucked a long-bladed knife from an unseen sheath.

A line of prisoners on work detail passed the alley. Nicole almost cried aloud as she recognized two of the men from the ship's company, who now carried shovels and pitchforks. They looked bedraggled, filthy, and hungry.

A guard flanking the final prisoners took one step into the alley, then another. John Jackson moved up alongside him and used his free hand to place something into the soldier's hand. Nicole heard the clink of sovereigns, followed by a quiet hiss from the soldier.

Clearly one of the final prisoners had been waiting for just that signal. He stepped into the alley, where instantly Jackson pulled him into the shadows beside Nicole.

The guard whispered, "Ten seconds only, or I'll be swinging alongside the captain."

The bosun's face was alight beneath his coating of grime and fatigue. "Miss Nicole!"

"Oh, Carter, whatever are we to do?"

"I wish I could tell you, ma'am. But whatever it is, you'll need to be moving fast. The captain is to breakfast with the hangman at dawn."

"Soldiers!" The guard reached and yanked on Carter's sleeve. "Move!"

Carter shook the man's hand away. "Get in touch with us through the guard here. He's a good enough sort."

The guard said frantically, "Come now—or it's both our necks!"

Nicole moved toward Jackson, who had anticipated her thought and had the purse ready. She took the purse and gave it to Carter. "Tell Gordon I will do my utmost."

Chapter 26

A new guard came along to release Gordon for the evening meal. He gave his prisoner a sideways glance, nothing much in and of itself. But something in the cast of the man's eyes, or perhaps the way his lips folded in upon themselves, raised Gordon's heart rate. He was alert and ready for the new light he spotted in Carter's gaze.

The bosun and his remaining men were well accustomed by now to forming a human barrier around Gordon. They moved as one toward the steaming barrel of gruel, shuffling along with the other prisoners, blocking Carter's quietly spoken announcement, "I spoke with Miss Nicole."

Gordon felt the words as a lance straight into his heart.

The bosun had clearly been expecting this, for he gripped Gordon's arm and drew him forward by his own strength. "Steady, sir," he murmured, lips barely moving. "There's only one set of eyes we can trust among the guards, and him only so long as our gold holds out."

Gordon nodded. "What did she say?"

"That she would try to help us. And you were to know that she would do her utmost."

Gordon fought off the urge to shout, to sing out loud. "Carter, this news has lifted me up to the heavens."

"Aye, sir, I thought you'd be pleased. I reckon we'll see results of her handiwork any moment now."

"Hold there." Gordon's sudden lightheartedness left him able to speak of doom with calm and directness. "We are friends, Carter. And at such a time as this, friends should not be anything less than clear with one another."

Carter frowned. "But Miss Nicole is a lady of pluck and determination, sir."

"That she is. But against her is arrayed the might of the entire British garrison." Gordon moved a manacled arm toward the ramparts with all their guards and muskets. "You said yourself, we have one guard only on our side. In a year, with her connections and her resolve, Miss Nicole might work wonders. But in fourteen hours?"

"I won't give up . . . I dare not," Carter said grimly. He reached into his pocket and pulled out Nicole's purse. "The lady gave this to me."

"And so you must keep it." Gordon patted the man's sinewy arm. "I rely on you to keep up the men's spirits, and see to their needs until she comes to your aid."

"Oh, sir, you cannot give up hope." Carter's exclamation was full of pain.

"On the contrary," Gordon replied with a calm he knew was not his own. "I have had my first glimpse of eternity. Hope is what I feast upon this very hour."

Chapter 27

Nicole took special care with her dressing and her preparations. After so long on the road and living under less than gentle conditions, all the fashions of polite society seemed alien now. She moved at a slower pace than usual as her mind raced ahead. She framed a picture of what the night might look like. She placed herself in the chamber among the swirling throng and the brilliant talk, the bright music and the rich food. She tried to form the words she knew she would have to speak. The images were no problem, and the words she could at least begin to hear herself say. But when she stopped and imagined what might come next, her mind became blank. No amount of prayer could change this sense of stepping into the darkest night of the unknown.

A knock on the door signaled an end to her reverie. "Yes?"

The words were muffled through her door. "The carriage is here and ready, my lady."

She wished she had a large mirror so she could check her reflection. Taking a deep breath, she picked up her fan and small beaded bag, opened the door, and asked, "Did you have any trouble?"

"The alleyway is too tight for the carriage. . . ." John Jackson stopped and looked at her with astonishment.

"What is it, Jackson?"

He blinked. "My lady—well . . ."

"Yes?"

"If I had seen you like this at the beginning, I would have turned tail and headed for the hills." He grinned crookedly and took a step back. "You—you seem like a vision out of a book of fairy tales."

Nicole nodded her thanks and moved carefully down the stairs in her high corked heels. She turned the stairwell's corner and found herself facing Pastor Collins and a group of seminarians, all of whom stared silently at her. Nicole took the last step and then lifted the hem of her dress to give the reverend a formal curtsy. "I remain forever indebted to you, sir. For what you have instructed me during my first visit and also for the welcome you have graced me with in these very difficult times."

The pastor's unkempt hair grew like a fragile silver-white halo around his balding head. Plump cheeks beneath eyebrows that looked as though they needed trimming with garden shears, and his black garb was much the worse for wear. Yet his eyes shone with life and genuine care, leaving Nicole not only humbled but feeling inspired.

"My dear," Pastor Collins declared, "I could not be more proud if I had raised you myself."

Nicole had planned her wardrobe very carefully and had chosen for this night the dress she had worn for her last formal event in England. The skirt, shoulders, and sleeves were layer upon layer of crinoline and lace, each a different shade of ivory, mere traces of color removed from pure white. Her faux vest of midnight blue silk velvet accented the curve of her waist with an arrowhead of color at the front and back. Seed pearls formed the buttons, two rows, with another half dozen at each wrist and up the side of her high collar. Her only jewelry was the emerald pendant that had once belonged to Charles's mother. Nicole reached for Pastor Collins's hand. "Thank you, dear friend. And for your prayers. It is the prayers of you, my parents, my family, and my friends that go with me tonight. Would you be so kind as to escort me outside?"

A student held the door as the old reverend led Nicole to the waiting hired carriage. The driver scrambled down to doff his hat and say, "Your pardon, miss. I didn't expect such as this, coming from the seminary as you are."

"Thank you for waiting."

Jackson held the door as Pastor Collins helped Nicole take her seat. When the driver climbed back to his perch, the pastor leaned through the open door. "You will forgive me for saying it, but you seem strangely preoccupied for a lovely young lady stepping out for a fine night with royalty." Jackson nodded his agreement.

Nicole hesitated, then decided she would reveal to these men what she had planned. "I intend to offer the commandant my entire holdings," she announced softly. "My land, my goods, my jewelry. Everything I have, in exchange for Gordon's life."

Pastor Collins gripped her hand. "My dear Nicole!"

"I have no choice." She clenched his hand, willing herself not to shed a tear and ruin her carefully made-up face. "They will be hanging Gordon at dawn."

"This may be only foolhardy," Pastor Collins cautioned, his expression serious.

"The reverend is right, ma'am. It would not help your captain one whit," John Jackson solemnly said. "You must put this out of your mind."

"If the commandant had the slightest inkling that you are a rebel sympathizer," the pastor explained, "he would confiscate everything you own without hesitation!"

"Lower your voice, Reverend," Jackson cautioned.

"Forgive me." Pastor Collins spoke more softly but held back none of the urgency. "If ever you have listened to me, Nicole, heed me now. Do not take this course."

"I cannot simply sit by and let him hang!"

"Softly, now, softly." Jackson scouted the road. "The night has ears."

"What am I to do, then?" Nicole asked.

"On this matter, I can offer only prayer," Pastor Collins replied, glancing behind him at the light spilling from the seminary's open doorway. "There are too many others whom God has placed in my care."

"Then pray your hardest, Reverend," John Jackson said grimly.

Nicole's nodded agreement was all she could manage.

Chapter 28

The commandant's formal chambers were full of lively talk and the glitter of military power. The front staircase, reception area, and the hall leading to the banquet room were all lined with hussars in elaborate uniforms, the chin straps of their helmets cocked just below their mouths. Nicole had but a brief instant to meet the commandant and his wife in the receiving line before she was swept into the long formal gallery. There the officers regaled each other and their ladies with boasts of how they intended to make the rebel forces suffer. Sabers hanging from the officers' belts rattled with each gesture. Brightly gowned ladies spoke of a time when all this would be behind them, after the colonists had been taught a lesson and put in their proper place.

The banquet table seemed as long as a sailing vessel and sat four dozen to a side. White-gloved hussars brought an endless array of dishes, none of which Nicole was able to more than taste. To her right was seated a cavalry officer, on her left a beribboned general from the New York regiments. The conversation was all of battles won.

Finally there came the moment when all rose and offered the final toast to the Prince of Wales. The men then retired to the smoking chamber, while the women gathered over tea and biscuits. Nicole saw the commandant's wife moving toward her and once again wondered if she should heed or ignore the advice of John Jackson and Pastor Collins.

"My dear viscountess, forgive me for not speaking with you before, but in this crush of people, my goodness, I was trapped."

"Of course. I understand fully." Frantically Nicole said a silent prayer. What was she to do?

"Why, you must certainly have faced the same dilemma on countless occasions." A large woman, the commandant's wife had a voice no doubt accustomed to running an immense household. Her eyes were as steely gray as her hair. "When were you last in England?" she asked.

"I departed from there in November."

"What I would give to return to civilization and put all this . . ." She swept the thought aside with an impatient wave of her fan. "Perhaps you had the opportunity to meet my father, Lord Cheswick."

"Forgive me, I do not recall such an honor."

"Oh, well, perhaps not. He is getting on in years and doesn't get about as much as he used to." She signaled a hovering waiter and commanded, "Tea and cakes for two."

"Immediately, my lady."

She turned back to Nicole. "Where have you managed to secure rooms, Viscountess?"

"At the hostel run by the Anglican seminary."

The commandant's wife looked startled. "But, but . . . is that not by the waterfront?"

"Indeed it is." Nicole knew she should be thinking more swiftly, formulating a plan. But her mind was a jumble of frenzied thoughts with no clear path whatsoever. "I had an introduction there. And I did not find other accommodations."

"Then we shall most certainly correct that matter, or I shall know the reason why." She snapped her fan shut.

"Your accent, my dear viscountess, it is quite delicious. Wherever were you born?"

Before Nicole could form a proper response, the commandant's wife was interrupted by an approaching officer. "Well, what is it?" she demanded.

"My lady, please forgive me," the man said as he bowed to the commandant's wife. He then turned to Nicole and asked, "Are you the Viscountess Harrow?"

"Yes, I am."

"Your manservant is at the front door, my lady. He says it is urgent."

Nicole thankfully rose to her feet. "Please excuse me, madame."

She followed the officer down the great hall. Seemingly watching her progress was an endless line of glowering military portraits. Whatever John Jackson had to say, she decided then and there, she would not return to the ball afterward. Her helplessness left her almost unable to place one foot in front of the next. The dawn and Gordon's imminent death felt but a few heartbeats away.

"Are you well, my lady?"

"Where is my manservant?"

"He awaits you by the outer portico."

Nicole passed by the flanking guards and reentered the night. The sky was so clear the stars nearly outshone the torches along the commandant's entryway. John Jackson stood on the bottom stair, and when she appeared in the doorway, he swept the hat from his head. But the closer she came, the farther he backed away, until they were standing between two carriages, partially blocked from view.

"My apologies, my lady, for not waiting inside," Jackson said. "But I could not see myself surrounded by so many redcoats."

"I understand. What is it?"

"I may have found our contact. Can you take your leave now?"

Nicole started down the lane. "Yes, I have no intention of entering that place again."

He led her to an empty carriage near the main entrance and then opened and held the door for her. "I have bribed the driver to let me take you from here. I fear your reputation may suffer as a result. He thinks you—he believes you may be headed for an illicit assignation."

"Never mind that. Time is slipping by us!"

"Softly, my lady. Softly." Jackson shut her door and climbed up. Gripping the reins, he clicked the horses into motion. Nicole resisted the urge to lean out the window and tell him to race to wherever it was they were going. She had to trust him. She had no other choice. Even so, the man's pace was maddeningly slow. She could almost hear the seconds tick away, and at far faster a pace than the plodding horses.

In a flash she learned the reason for their studied pace. As they passed a narrow lane, a figure rushed up alongside, swung open the carriage door, and leaped aboard. "Well done, my fair lassie! Well done, indeed."

The carriage rocked precariously under the new passenger's large frame, with a paunch that threatened to split his shirt. His leer revealed more gaps than yellow teeth. His cheeks bore a week's stubble, and his eyes glittered. "That's a fancy bit of fluff you're wearing, lassie," he said familiarly.

Nicole drew herself against the far door. "Who are you?"

"Ah now, that's not a question you need to be asking, is it? The only question you want answering is, 'What can I do for your fancy Gordon Goodwind?'"

The carriage rounded a corner and entered a silent dark square. Instantly Jackson reined in the horses, threw on the brake, and leaped to the ground. He opened the door beside Nicole. Although he didn't step inside, his proximity gave Nicole the strength to say, "Captain Gordon Goodwind is not—."

"Ah, so you'll be taking this risk just because he's of a good sort, is that it?"

"Precisely so."

His eyes disappeared into the folds of his face. "A likely tale, that is. But I wasn't born yesterday. Nor the day before."

Jackson rapped out, "The lady's reasons are her own."

"Aye, true enough. Long as she's willing to meet my price, she can sing whatever tune she likes." The glittering eyes traced their way down her dress. "And my price is a high one, I can tell you that."

"Price for what?" said Nicole sharply.

John Jackson replied, "This man claims to be the assistant messcook for the prison stockade."

"Where did you find him?"

"In the foulest tavern this side of Blighty," the cook laughed.

"The guard who helped us this afternoon," Jackson explained. "He led me there. I owe him for the service."

Without taking her eyes off the man seated opposite, Nicole removed the pouch from her purse. "Here. Pay him what you must."

The cook's eyes darted from Nicole to the pouch and back again. "It'll be taking more than that for me to risk life and limb," he said.

"You don't even know how much it is."

"It's not enough, I can tell you that." He lifted one grimy finger and pointed to the emerald pendant hanging around her neck. "That bauble there, now, and three pouches stuffed to the gullets with finest King Georgies. That should see me just fine."

"Are you mad!" Jackson exploded.

"Aye, that may well be. Mad enough to help yon lassie

slip her fancy man past a stockade guard."

Nicole saw John Jackson stiffen with rage. "Wait. Please." To the cook she said, "Your price is absurdly high, sir."

"I'm no sir, lass. But I know what I want." He jerked a thumb out the window. "I want quit of all this. I want enough to see me set up with land and a farm of my very own. And either you're my ticket, or I'll be walking back to join my maties and have myself another mug."

"It is too high," Nicole insisted, while at the same time forcing herself to remain steady and calm. "For just the one man."

This was clearly not what the cook expected. "Eh, what's that?"

"I agree to meet your price. But only if you bring out not just Captain Goodwind but all his men as well."

"All—?"

"Ten sailors plus Gordon. They are set to be lashed and press-ganged. Gordon will want them to be saved from that fate." She could hardly believe the calm she was hearing in her own voice. "Do that and I shall not pay you three sacks of sovereigns but five."

The cook was no longer smiling. "And the bauble there?"

"This emerald pendant, yes. Five sacks of gold sovereigns plus my necklace. Do we have an agreement?"

His eyes shifted from one face to the other. "How do I know you'll pay what you owe?"

Chapter 29

The camp had finally settled and the air grew quiet, yet Gordon remained once more awake. Other than at mealtime, there was little activity around him. Feeling perpetually worn down had more to do with his confinement than anything else—that and the weariness which comes from never being truly warm or dry or fed. Through the barred window and door, Gordon could hear groans of men wrestling with the elusiveness of sleep.

Then he heard the sound again from next door. The young man destined to hang with him the following morning, the hungry soldier convicted of stealing a lady's purse. He attempted to swallow his sobs.

"Harry," Gordon whispered. "I say there, Harry."

There was a moment's silence, then the young man's whimpered, "Sir?"

Gordon slid off his bedding and moved as close to the side wall as his chains allowed. "No need for titles here, lad. They've all been stripped away. The name is Gordon."

"G-Gordon." The swallow was so loud it sounded through the wall. "I'm . . . afraid."

"Aye." He leaned back against the wall. "You know I'm to hang with you."

"I know."

"That makes us brothers of a sort, wouldn't you say?"

Gordon rubbed a sore spot on his shoulder against the rough mortar, his chains clinking with each motion. He had accepted with the coming of night that there was nothing Nicole or anyone could do to change the course of events. Were he held for months or years, then her sway as a viscountess might have altered things. But military justice during wartime was as swift as it was merciless. "It helps to know we're not going to climb those stairs alone."

"I . . . I suppose."

The silence was a comfortable one now. Gordon took a long breath. It seemed to him as if he stood at the apex of something utterly new. A door opened before him, one that the chains could not keep him from entering. Not these chains, nor even this earth. "Would you like to pray with me, lad? One brother with another?"

———— ❧ ————

Gordon's senses had been trained by years of constant vigilance while at sea. A shift in the wind, a change in the tide's running, these and many others marked time for him as precisely as the ticking of a clock. Even though it was still black as ink outside his window, the sky blanketed with thick clouds and the air filled with a stationary mist, he knew that dawn was not far off. Young Harry had drifted to sleep hours before. He, however, hadn't budged from his spot against the wall. He found comfort in listening to the young man breathe as he slept. But more than this, Gordon found a rightness to it, too, as though the act of praying with him had brought them so close he could care for him as he might a son—a son he would now never have.

Moments later, while the mist crept in and obscured what little light might have entered from the torches and campfires, Gordon's own internal vistas remained brilliant and clear. He sat there with his eyes opened wide and stared straight ahead. But what he saw was far behind, all the way back to his early days on the open sea.

He recalled the moment when he stood on the quarterdeck as captain of his own vessel for the very first time. It had been a magnificent day. He had risen with the dawn watch and ordered the men to send aloft all sails. The rising canvas had snapped and caught the wind and drawn up tight—billows of white that ascended ninety feet and more. Leaping forward, the ship cleaved the sea like a great wooden ax. An albatross then appeared as if from nowhere and hung there alongside his head, its wings motionless. The sun had emerged behind him, turning the great bird into a phoenix of flames and eternal beginnings, and the sea into crimson and gold and white. From the mainmast's pinnacle, the watchkeeper had piped with his pocket fife a merry salute to the break of day, to all new days everywhere. And it had seemed to Gordon that this was as fine as life could be, sailing toward a boundless horizon, aboard a ship filled with jolly Jack-tars, with nothing ahead of him but a wealth of adventure.

In his cell Gordon detected a whisper of sound, but he resisted releasing the vision. Instead he lifted his eyes toward the roof. *I have never thanked thee for that dawn,* he confessed. *In fact, I have never acknowledged thy place in it at all. But I see thee there now, Father. And I thank thee.*

The sound drew closer still until soon there was the sibilant rustle of metal on metal, and his cell door was pushed gently open. Two shadows flitted inside without benefit of torch or lantern. Gordon watched them with the calm of one who had already taken his leave and observed, "It is not yet time."

"Quiet, you. For all our sakes," hissed a stranger's voice. "Where's the latch to your wall chains?"

Chapter 30

Not even after his ankle chains dropped away and he took his first free step in days could Gordon believe it was actually happening. Not even after the jailer thrust a moth-eaten red coat into his hands and rasped out, "Put this on."

But then he stepped outside the cell to see Carter grinning there before him and heard the man breathe, "God bless the lady, sir. God *bless* her."

Gordon felt his heart grow wings and leap from the gallows. "Nicole?"

"Who else? We—"

A hiss silenced them both. They were pressed over to the stockade's east wall, where the cluster of men grew one by one. Soon all Gordon's mates were there with him, smiling and rubbing wrists and ankles, barely able to take in the fact that they might be making a run for it.

The jailer came by once more and handed out ragged soldiers' coats to each of the prisoners. Gordon stepped forward, grasped the jailer's arm, and whispered, "There's one more."

"Ten plus you. That was the—"

"Eleven," Gordon said and drew him over to the door next to his own. "Here."

The jailer seethed but then did as he was bidden. It

was dreadful entering death's cage again, but Gordon steeled himself and moved forward with the jailer. The clink of chains signaled that Harry was awake. This was followed by the soft cry of terror.

"Quiet now, lad."

"Gordon?"

———— ❧ ————

They waited by the stockade's inner gates for what seemed eons, but in fact was less than an hour. The morning gathered slowly, as though night itself were trapped within the heavy fog's grip and kept there long against its will. The air clogged tight with a cold wetness, and several men buried their heads in their borrowed greatcoats to stifle coughs.

Two jailers stood with them, the ones Carter had pointed out the previous day as having aided in talking to Nicole. They were a brutish pair, and it left Gordon with a foul taste to have to put himself in the hands of soldiers who could be bought.

Harry turned out to be a goodly enough fellow, lean in the way of many foot soldiers who didn't have enough coin to add to their meager diet. Tall, he had the reddish blond hair of good English stock. In the faint light Gordon could see how his eyes had retreated back into dark caves, from which they now watched the dawn with feverish intensity. Clearly he still feared he would more than likely be cut off from breath and life in but an hour's time.

The morning's first thrush chirped in the distance. Gordon took this as a signal of hope. Beyond the wooden stockade walls came a faint murmuring, sleepy men reaching the end of a cold night's watch. The jailers exchanged anxious looks. Gordon then gave a single nod and a flicker of hand motions, and the men moved with haste into double file. Prisoners they might be, with limbs weak as water, but they had lived and breathed military precision all their lives. Their hats and coats were the dregs, taken from the military mess. Not even the poorest soldier would be inclined to try to repair the many holes, most of which were surrounded by dark stains. Two of the hats were missing corners. But in the murky half-light, with the mist draped over everything, hopefully they could pass unnoticed.

They stepped forward, marching in weary unison. One of the jailers called, "Open up, you!"

"Who goes down there?" The mist thickened until it was almost impossible to make out the figure who peered at them from the stockade parapet. Gordon knew that with the sun rising behind him, it was unlikely the man would see anything at all.

"That you, Derek?" asked the jailer.

"Who else would be out in this gloom and cold?"

Try as he might, the jailer couldn't keep his voice from skittering up and down. "Open the door and let us get to our beds."

"There's a good half hour left to the watch." The figure overhead shifted to one side. "Light the torch, will you? I can't see my hand before my face."

"Couldn't. Everything down here is wet as rainwater. Open the door, I tell you."

Reluctantly the guard moved toward the latch, then suddenly stepped back and said, "Where's your officer of the watch, then?"

Gordon felt the night press down, the gloom holding them tightly in place. Their way forward was blocked, and he could do nothing to break free. Nothing, except . . .

His heart thundering, he slipped back a few paces and then came stomping forward. In his sternest quarterdeck voice he rapped out, "What's the holdup here?"

The two jailers jerked backward in surprise, and the

soldier overhead snapped to attention and said, "Begging pardon, sir. But it's not time yet for the watch change."

"Indeed not! But we have a nasty business ahead of us today, and I want the graves dug and the preparations in order before the prison comes to life!"

"Right you are, sir." The soldier ran down and unlatched the inner gates. Tugging on the rope, he swung the door open wide. He then turned and barked, "You there, open the outer gates! Officer and his men coming through."

Chapter 31

The stockade was situated on the boggy terrain that separated the marshland from the pasture now housing the British garrison. As light strengthened to the east, the hills of Boston rose up like islands in a distant golden sea. The mist clung tight to the earth yet lifted with each footfall, surrounding the marching men with mystery and safety.

They passed by the first cluster of houses, inns, and taverns that catered to the foot soldiers. Then, where a narrow lane split and led to some farm dwellings, a man stepped from behind a tree and whistled once.

"That's our man," the jailer said. Relief and the tense march caused his breath to catch in his throat.

"Make haste, men," Gordon murmured. "Double time."

The men trotted over to where the stranger stood waving urgently. They turned the corner to find a rope line holding the reins of fifteen horses. The stranger counted swiftly, then hissed, "We're one horse shy!"

Gordon demanded, "Who might you be?"

"John Jackson is the name. In the employ of the finest woman I have ever had the honor to meet." He offered his hand. "And you, sir, are a most fortunate man."

Gordon accepted the man's grip. "Aye, I can't argue with you there."

Off in the distance behind them could be heard the tinny trumpet sound of alarm. "Fly!" John Jackson leaped into the saddle of the nearest horse. "For the sake of the Lady Nicole, fly like the wind!"

Gordon mounted his horse and then pulled Harry up behind him. "Can you ride?"

"Since I was eight."

"Then hold tight and lean into me!"

They careened out of cover and thundered down the empty road heading west, away from both Boston and the soldiers. Over the sound of pounding hooves, Gordon thought he heard musket fire, though it might well have been his imagination. John Jackson was ten lengths ahead and pulling away fast. Carter and two of the other men slowed to stay apace of Gordon's doubly laden horse, but then Gordon waved them forward. "Hold hard to our guide!" he shouted.

They raced through a fog that seemed to part before them and close up behind. Three times Gordon glanced behind them and could make out nothing but a brilliant white veil. Then he stopped looking back, for it caused his laboring horse to falter. Instead he leaned down till his chin rested on the horse's nape and shouted, "Hyah!"

They galloped on until he could hear the horse's breath rasping raw and he could sense the legs carrying them begin to weaken. The closest man to them was now so far ahead Gordon could only see but a faintly shifting shadow. John Jackson and the front-runners were lost to the fog and the distance. Gordon was about to call to the men and order them to continue on without him, when the man ahead reined in and turned sharply to the left, leaving behind the river and marsh. Thankfully Gordon did the same. A narrow track opened and began snaking through the trees. His horse was stumbling heavily now. Harry slipped off the back and said, "I'll run from here."

"Well done, lad. We'll wait for you farther on."

A half mile ahead, the forest gave way to raw pasture-land. Gordon then spied a ramshackle house, obviously no longer occupied. A huge man stood awaiting them. John Jackson strode from his horse to the porch. Gordon rushed forward and, to his astonishment, realized he was facing the stockade's cook.

"That's far enough!" the cook said, showing them the business end of a loaded musket. "Now I'll be seeing either the color of your wares or your innards."

"First show me that the lady is in good straights," demanded Jackson.

Gordon dismounted and stepped forward. "What's this?" he asked.

"It was the Lady Nicole's idea," Jackson explained as the cook moved to the door and shoved it open. "We could not pay until you were free. But we had to prove to them we would do as we promised."

"She gave herself as hostage?"

Jackson was a tall man, almost matching Gordon's height, and had the look of one who knew how to handle himself in a fight. "For you, yes," he said with a challenging stare.

"Gordon!"

The young woman who stepped through the doorway was, in Gordon's eyes, the most beautiful of God's creations. He was there in a flash, holding himself in check as he grasped both of her outstretched hands.

"Oh, thank the good Lord above!" exclaimed Nicole, gazing into his eyes as her own filled with tears.

"Amen," he said, and for the first time he felt he was well and truly free. "Amen."

"Yes, all the amens are fine," the cook sneered. "Now let's be seeing the payment."

John Jackson reached into his saddlebags and came out with three heavy purses. The jailers eagerly received theirs.

Gordon was shocked. "Are those sovereigns?"

In reply the jailers untied the purses and spilled a flow of gold into their hands.

Gordon protested, "But that is more than I earned from the entire ship's voyage!"

"Let's be having the rest, then," said the cook, his hand outstretched.

Gordon watched as John Jackson pulled two more purses from a different saddlebag and handed them over.

The cook waited till all the contents had been inspected, then demanded, "And the bauble?"

Reluctantly Jackson took a handkerchief from his coat pocket and held it out toward the cook. The man walked forward, slipped back the folds, and lifted out the emerald pendant. "There's my beauty."

Gordon started forward but was halted by Nicole's hand on his arm. He looked into her eyes and felt the anger fade. She said nothing, but he understood.

"Aye, this here's enough to see us well rid of stamping and saluting and other men's wars." The cook pulled himself into the saddle, waited for his two mates to mount up, then gave the group a final leering grin. "Looks like some of you lot will just have to hoof it."

Nicole straightened and said, "Go with God, sir."

All three men stared at her from their saddles. The cook responded with a mock salute, and then he and the jailers rode off without looking back.

Chapter 32

Their progress was as swift as could be, given the men's exhausted state. They each took turns walking or trotting alongside the horses carrying those fortunate enough to ride. The weather remained with them, however, and blanketed the road with a mist so heavy the whole world appeared as myriad shades of gray. Keeping to the roadside and off the main trail, the men forged ahead, being careful to stay nearby the sheltering woodlands.

At one point they happened upon a company of men and so, just in time, disappeared out of sight. The soldiers rode by like fierce shadows, officers on stallions prancing before and after. Hands clamped around their own mount's jaws, Gordon's men didn't breathe till the sound of the horses had drifted into the gray and windless distance.

Before long Jackson led them into a forest that cut between the road and the river. They stopped for a short rest and to drain the single canteen, just enough for a few swallows each. Jackson said, "The Charles River is over a mile wide at this point. Either we find us a boat or we will be forced to send some men back to Boston to steal one."

Gordon's frown was the only response. "You have an idea where we might find us a vessel?"

"I might. Although *vessel* is hardly the term I would use."

"If it floats, it will serve us." Gordon rose wearily to his feet and signaled to his men. "Lead on."

The Boston side of the Charles River was lined not with a proper bank but with marshland that made it difficult to tell precisely where the river began. Muddy grasslands spread in patches wider than the river itself. How John Jackson could find his way back through the fog, thick marsh and woods, Nicole would never understand. To her, the low-hanging branches and foul water all seemed identical. But Jackson guided them onward, every step taking them farther into the muck. She kept hoping to see some measure of a trail that might look familiar. It wasn't until they came to the natural corral, where the trees formed a kind of overhanging tent, that she could say with certainty, "We have arrived." She looked around for the boat in which she had previously crossed the river at this same location.

The men let out sighs of relief, and Gordon said, "Well done, sir. I say, well done."

"Let us hope the boat is on this side," Jackson said, sliding from his horse. "Else all will have been for naught."

Gordon joined Jackson in searching for the launch. Quickly the men unsaddled the horses, but they abruptly stopped, heads up. At first Nicole couldn't determine what had alerted them. Then she heard it. The faint sound of a trumpet. The baying of hounds.

John Jackson and Gordon must have heard it as well, for they came rushing back through the thicket. Breathing hard, Gordon announced, "The vessel is there. But she will not hold us all."

"But we can't delay, not by a minute!" said Jackson. "They will be on us in a flash."

"You are certainly right about that. I have hunted with hounds and have seen how swift they can move." Gordon's forehead creased. "There is but one way out of this."

John Jackson nodded sharply. "I recall seeing some rope in the corral."

"Good man." Gordon motioned the others toward the river. "Let's be off."

Nicole waited until they were near the boat before asking, "Gordon, what is happening?"

"We will put our stoutest oarsmen in the boat. The others will hold on to lines and swim with all their might." Gordon pointed to Carter and three others. "You there. Leave room in the bow for Nicole."

"No," she protested. "I will swim as well."

"My dear, that is quite out of the question. The river still holds to winter's chill."

"And there are men here who are nearly falling down with fatigue." She gestured to the tall young stranger who stood with arms wrapped around his chest, leaning against a tree. "Look at that one there."

"Yes, I had thought Harry could perhaps steer the boat." Gordon called to him, "Lad, can you handle a tiller?"

"I fished with my father since I was a small boy," he answered. He made a feeble attempt to straighten himself. "But I can swim, sir."

"No doubt," Gordon said kindly. "But today we shall require your skill at the helm."

John Jackson appeared then, two large coils of rope over his shoulder. "I believe the hounds have gotten wind of our scent!"

"Let's be off. We've no time to waste."

"Beg pardon, sir," Carter said. "We've got two men who cannot swim, and both are too weak to do much on the oars. And another has a festering shoulder wound."

Gordon rubbed his forehead. Nicole knew how very few seamen could swim. The opinion of those belowdecks was that, with the seas being so vast, learning to stay afloat would only postpone the inevitable. Better still was never to get wet. This knowledge caused her to declare, "Gordon, please, I must insist."

Gordon studied her, then said, "I have no cause to order you about. But I must warn you, if you fall away there is nothing any of us can do."

"I understand."

"All right then." He turned back to his men. Choosing those worst off would be next to impossible, for all were haggard from the experience of the past few days. "Which others of you cannot swim a lick?"

Two more raised their hands.

"That settles it. You'll bend your backs to the oars instead."

Jackson pulled two battered paddles from the underbrush. "They can ply these and speed our crossing," he said.

"A measure of good fortune," said Gordon, adding, "If there were only a canoe to go along with those." As the men tied the ropes to either side of the stern, Gordon said to Carter, "You are in charge. Row with all your might. When you grow too tired, change over. No heroics, just strong and steady."

"We won't fail you, sir."

"We're counting on precisely that." He clapped the bosun on the shoulder and said to the others, "Give yourselves plenty of space. No bunching up. We'll lash you about the middles. You'll need to hold the line with one hand and push hard with the other."

"Off with your gear," John Jackson instructed. "Overcoats and boots and belts. The works. Toss it all into the river."

Without being asked, Nicole shed her outer mantle and vest. She did as the others and rolled up the excess clothing. Stepping into the river, she flung the bundle as far out as she could. She bit her lip to stifle the gasp when the water came up around her knees. It felt as if tiny blades of ice were raking her skin.

She walked over to where Gordon was fashioning a loop and let him fit it around her waist. "Don't rely on the loop alone, for it may become too tight and cut off your breathing," he said.

"I won't fail you either, Gordon."

Fitting his own loop around his body, Gordon smiled. "Of that, my dear Nicole, I have no doubt whatsoever."

They paused then, all of them staring out to where the river faded into the mist. There was no way of determining the distance, nor aiming exactly for their destination. All of them knew a moment's shared fear, of wishing they could turn back. But behind them they could hear the barking of hounds. The fog and marsh played tricks on their hearing, for one moment it sounded as though the dogs were yet a mile or two away, the next they seemed just out of sight.

"Everyone ready?" Gordon said, his voice light and measured.

Together they launched the vessel, allowing the oarsmen and the fast-flowing current to draw them away. Nicole could not suppress a small cry as the water rose higher—to her waist, chest, and then neck. The cold took hold of her. Ahead the oarsmen pulled hard, while the two men in the bow dug deep with the canoe paddles. Nicole was standing and walking farther out when suddenly her feet were swept out from under her, followed by a wave flipping over her face. She went under and came up gasping for breath.

"Swim!" Gordon called out from behind her. "Stay warm and keep the boat from dragging so!"

She would never be warm again. The water reached with merciless fingers through her skin and pierced her lungs, her very bones. She swam, yet could feel a heavy lethargy spreading throughout her body. The only thing encouraging was the speed at which the water shot past her. Those with the oars and paddles strained, each stroke bringing steady grunts of effort as they attempted to drag forward the water-borne train.

From the riverbank where they had launched came a harsh shout and then muskets fired. Nicole could not turn around and didn't know if they could be seen or if the British soldiers were merely firing into the fog. Concentrating on the one vital task of swimming was all she could do. She kicked her legs and felt the dress wrap tightly about her body like a trap. With her free hand she forced herself to pull forward. The pain in her other arm and wrist where the line was coiled was almost welcome because it made her alert. It helped her to focus and breathe, to keep swimming.

But despite her hardest efforts, the cold continued to sap her strength, entering her lungs with each breath and penetrating her muscles. The weight of her sopping dress dragged her down and caused her limbs to ache. Soon she was left with hardly any feeling at all.

Each breath now ended in a tight muffled sob. She could hear herself make these noises, though her mind seemed unable to accept they were originating from her. Catching sight of the men in the boat, how they strained and fought, she realized at one point that the oarsmen had switched positions. Those who had before been leaning against the oars were now slumped over their benches, so drained they couldn't hold their heads upright.

Where were they? Had they reached the midway point? Each question formed more slowly, the cold now working its way into her mind so even thoughts occurred to her as impossibly heavy.

Nicole heard the men in the boat let out a cry. She saw Harry turn from his position at the tiller and shout out words to them in the water. But she couldn't make out what the sounds meant. It was all too much bother to her.

Then her feet brushed up against something. The opposite bank. But she was unable to draw her legs up under herself. Ahead of her, men leaped from the boat into the river. She knew this was important, that it signified something. Just what it was she couldn't say. All she could think of was how warm the water had become. How easy it would be to lower her head and let herself sink beneath the softly lapping waves, to drift away.

Strong hands grabbed her and hauled her forward. She opened her eyes, yet couldn't tell who it was that held her. Feeling tugs on the rope around her middle, she thought how this must hurt, but still she felt no pain.

She was pulled from the water by two men. They slipped the rope from around her before moving her farther up onto dry land. She struggled to move her arms, then legs. Again she felt nothing. She heard gasping and was frightened to realize it was her own. Then, as they laid her gently down on the grassy bank and rubbed her hands and feet, a new sensation arrived. The pain that struck her limbs was so fierce she almost wished she could return to the river. It was difficult even to cry out, for she began shivering violently, trembling so much that her breath came in clipped whimpers.

Nicole heard then what the men were saying. One of them—Carter was his name, she remembered this now—repeated the same words over and over. To her surprise it sounded like the man was crying. Which was impossible, she knew. Carter was a sailor, and such men never wept.

"Bless you, Miss Nicole. Bless you, ma'am! You've done the impossible. You've given us God's miracle. We're alive; we're here among free men. Bless you."

She wanted to ask about Gordon and to ask why Carter's face was wet, since he hadn't been in the river. But her eyelids felt as if pressed down by a great weight. Her last thought was an echo of Carter's words. *Miracle.*

Chapter 33

Nicole awoke to find herself surrounded by fire and warmth. The sun was struggling to come out from behind the fog and clouds, while to the left and right of her burned great campfires. She lifted her head and discovered Gordon seated by her feet, staring at her. The look in his eyes warmed her as much as the flames, perhaps more. "I was wrong," she said.

"Pardon me?"

"I thought I would never be warm again." Nicole tried to sit up and was grateful when he moved to aid her. "How is everyone?"

"Fine. We are fine. All of us safe and sound. Thanks to you." He handed her a cloth piled with bread and cheese. "John Jackson might have cast aside boots and belt, but he kept hold of your coin. He foraged this from a nearby farm."

Nicole took the bread with one hand and the cheese with the other but was restrained from devouring both instantly by Gordon's hands. "Steady there," he cautioned. "You've had a terrible shock. Take it slow and easy, that's my lady."

She did as she was told, though it was hard to chew and swallow and wait. The bread seemed the finest she had ever tasted, the cheese too. When the worst of her hunger had been averted, Nicole was able to look up at Gordon and search his face. What was he thinking?

Gordon stretched out his legs, easing muscles that were clearly still cramped from the day's exertions. "There's so much I need to tell you, Nicole," he said, his voice low.

"And I you. And so many questions."

"Then we shall take turns," he said. He smiled at her with features still taut with the woes and worries he'd been carrying. "As I watched you sleep, I found myself wishing the old reverend from the mission was here with us. I know him hardly at all, yet I was thinking he would be a good man to talk with right now. Someone who would listen with more than his ears. A man with a lifetime's worth of experience."

"He is all that," Nicole replied, "and more besides."

"To tell the truth, I wish for him now because I have much I would like to say to you, and I do not yet hold the proper words."

Nicole set aside what remained of her meal. Though she still felt hunger, she could not have anything else on her mind or within her vision just now. "Please try," she said.

"Very well." He stared at the flickering flames, and his voice crept lower still. "I should like to tell you of my dark night there in the prison. But not now. We must be off before much longer, and this event is too vital to be hurried in the telling. For now I must simply say that you were right, and I was wrong."

Nicole could not speak, but he seemed to understand and took up his narrative again.

"I have been brought to realize that strength taken to an extreme becomes a weakness. Anything which keeps me from relying upon God becomes a barrier to eternity. I am incomplete. I see that now. Being strong, even holding a leader's wisdom, does not end my need for what can only come through the divine." He looked at her then. "Forgive me. I have chosen my words very poorly."

"On the contrary, they are most meaningful and beautiful. I believe you now understand why faith is so vital to me." She looked away then, and she could feel his eyes studying her.

"What troubles you?" he asked finally.

Nicole looked directly at him. "I must ask you of how you came to be captured."

His gaze darkened, like a storm had become trapped in his eyes. "A mercenary working for the British led us straight into their waiting arms."

Nicole drew her legs up close and folded her stiff, dry dress around her. "Tell me about him."

"Acadian, like yourself. A tall man, strong, dark of hair and features. Has a small scar beneath his left eye." He must have seen alarm mounting in her eyes. "Do you know this man?"

"Perhaps . . ." She was panting again, as if different waters had reached out to grip her with a cold even fiercer than the river. "What—what was his name?"

"Henri Robichaud, he said. I will never forget it. Never."

From their small camp's perimeter, Jackson gave a quick shout. "Horses coming this way!"

Nicole rose with Gordon. "That was not Henri Robichaud."

Gordon was already searching the horizon. He turned quickly to her. "How can you be so certain?"

"Because," Nicole replied, "Henri Robichaud is my father."

Chapter 34

Gordon stared at her as horses thundered toward them. "But . . . you are a Harrow." He obviously was having trouble fitting his thoughts around her words. "He is too young to be your father."

"Henri Robichaud would never do such a thing as you described. Believe me on this, if ever you have believed me at all. I cannot explain it all now, but I am telling you the truth."

"Begging your pardon, sir," Carter said. "But perhaps you should call the men to arms."

"Arms? With what?" Gordon glanced in the direction of the approaching horses. "We have naught but our fists, and they that come are carrying lances and muskets both." Turning his attention back to Nicole, he asked her, "So who was it that betrayed me and my men?"

"I have much to tell you, so very much. My guesses will mean nothing until I have spoken with you fully. Believe me now when I say I wish to tell you everything, and that the man you met was *not* Henri Robichaud."

"I say!" The American officer rode a dappled stallion with a mane of silky black. The horse pranced and snorted when the officer reined it in. He used his saber and directed his men into two enfilades, which spread like arms to encircle the gathering. "Who might we have here?"

"Captain Gordon Goodwind, the Viscountess Lady Harrow, and a bevy of hardy soldiers seeking service under the banner of all free men." For once, Gordon's stiff bow lacked its customary finesse. He was barefoot and bedraggled, beltless and unshaven. "Your servant, sir."

"You don't say." The officer's mustache quivered with barely suppressed mirth. He cast a sardonic eye on Nicole, who was busy attempting to brush meadow grass and seaweed from her ruined dress. *At least I am dry*, she thought as she gathered up her tangled hair as best she could.

"A viscountess, did you say?"

"That is correct, sir. You must forgive our appearance. We have just recently escaped from the clutches of the British by swimming the river."

The officer's adjutant cleared his throat. "Excuse me, sir."

"A moment." The officer pointed with his saber to the bosun. "I bid you, lift your trouser leg."

Carter glanced at Gordon, whose jaw was knotted with tension, but who nodded agreement. Carter pulled up the hem of his pants, revealing coarsely abraded sores from the leg chains.

"You and your men are jail rats, I take it," the officer said, his humor now gone.

"Aye, sir, we were incarcerated by the British. We escaped because of the lady's help. We scarcely made it away with our lives." Then Gordon stopped speaking because the officer in charge was no longer listening. His adjutant had sidled his horse up close to the officer and was whispering intently.

"You don't say," the officer murmured. He turned back to Gordon, a new light in his eyes. "Goodwind, did you say?"

"Aye, sir. Gordon Goodwind."

"Well, you have some nerve, I will give you that." He motioned for his men to close in. "I can't say I quite understand your motives for returning, Captain. But you and your men are bound to trade one set of chains for another."

"You can't!" Nicole cried out. "These men have information that is vital to the American cause! You must take us to the garrison commandant."

"The men here are headed for the stockade. As for you"—the mustache quivered once more—"you are welcome to address the commandant if you wish. Although I imagine he has more important things on his mind than to have a camp follower join him for tea."

Gordon's men jerked forward with such ferocity the officer's steed snorted and pulled back. The opposing soldiers held their lances at the ready for attack. "Hold hard there!" Gordon roared, stilling his men's anger at the aspersion on Nicole's character.

Jackson quickly stepped forward and saluted. "Hard as it may be to believe, sir, these men are telling the truth. They were falsely accused as spies by both sides. But they are with us heart and soul."

"And just who," the officer grunted, "might you be?"

"John Jackson, sergeant with the Pennsylvania's Seventh."

"Then I shall arrest you for consorting with the enemy, which is a hanging offense."

Nicole was beside herself with anger and dismay. "This is absurd! You can't possibly think we would come up with such a preposterous—"

Gordon halted her with a hand on her arm. "You know the realities of wartime, my dear."

"But, Gordon—"

"There is nothing to be gained by a frontal attack," he countered, his words as much for his men as for her. "Do what you can, and come for us as swiftly as you are able."

Despite frustration and his weakened condition, he smiled with his eyes. "It appears I shall soon be placed even further in your debt."

"I will do anything——."

"Of that," he said, signaling his men into line, "I have no doubt."

Chapter 35

In spite of the overlong hike that left Gordon and his men limping badly, nothing seemed to affect his good humor. Gordon found reason to smile in the smallest of things. A robin saluted their passage, a warm southwesterly breeze blew aside the sky's final veil, and the pastures rippled with waves in greeting. When they stopped for a midday respite of well water, Gordon felt he had never tasted anything so fine. His men cast him questioning glances, and John Jackson eyed him with outright disbelief. Even the officer who stood nearby as they entered the stockade watched Gordon with a sideways glare.

Once they were processed and each handed a blanket and a tin meal bowl, Gordon threw himself down in a shadowy corner with only soiled hay for bedding. He watched the sky's two remaining clouds chase each other across a sea of open blue. He sighed with contentment. He was weary in his bones, yet for the moment his heart was too full to permit him to sleep.

John Jackson and Carter walked over together, bearing tins of gruel and battered cups of hot tea. "There's grub of a sort, Skipper."

"Well done, Carter. I fear my belly is becoming far too well acquainted with my backbone."

The two men looked at Gordon with the uncertainty

of mates left out of a good joke. Carter said hesitantly, "The men were wondering if you—well, if you are all right, sir."

"Never been better." Which, given the circumstances, was good for a chuckle.

"What Carter here means to say," added Jackson, "is we're wondering what it is that has you in such fine fettle."

"Well, let's see." Gordon pivoted around so that his back rested against the stockade's timber-and-wattle wall. Across the yard, two soldiers walked the parapet with muskets in their hands. But not even the sight of more armed guards could negate the fact that at least here he sat with mates to either side and a beautiful blue sky overhead. "I'm no longer bound for the gallows," he said. "And none of us are wearing chains."

Jackson pointed out, "But we *are* being held prisoner, and in the foulest stockade I've ever seen."

"Aye, but that's only because you haven't been where we last were," said Carter, catching a hint of his skipper's mood. "The British prison makes this one look like a field of posies and daffodils."

"And do not forget, we have an ally on the outside," Gordon said. "To speak personally, I'd rather have that solitary lady on our leeward side than a ship of the line with all her guns primed."

Carter grinned. "Truer words were never spoken, sir."

Gordon knew the moment demanded that he make one further confession. It heartened him to find the words coming steadily as he said, "And then there is the greatest gift of all, one I must also credit to Nicole. The gift of knowing that whatever I face, I do so with God and His Son."

John Jackson's expression was full of painful introspection. "I have many reasons to envy you, sir. But none so much as the ease with which you spoke those words."

Gordon reached over and gripped the man's arm. "At

least here I can offer you what I have, and only be enriched myself by the gift. For this gift was freely given, that I might share it with all who seek as I do."

At that moment, however, Gordon's confidence in her would only have made Nicole more miserable than she already was. When she presented herself to the sentries, they wouldn't permit her into the garrison compound, much less convey her name to someone at headquarters. "But I tell you, I am the Lady—"

"And I am telling *you* to be gone!" The sentry was growing red-faced, both because of her insistence and the way his mates were having a good laugh over his discomfort. "We don't want the likes of you consorting with our troops! Now off with you before I clamp you in the public stocks!"

Nicole could see he meant what he said and so fled in distress. She limped into town, the walk leaving her so footsore that even crossing the slick cobblestones proved painful. She was filthy, frustrated, and hungry. And she had not a single answer, nothing whatsoever she could think of that might change the circumstances. Gordon was once more behind bars, locked up like an animal, like the *enemy*. She felt helpless, without hope or a single complete thought, and so tired she couldn't form a decent prayer. She had only two empty hands reaching heavenward, a silent plea from a woman overwhelmed by the task in front of her.

"Excuse me, madame."

She was so weak that her turning around caused her to wince. "Do you speak with me, sir?"

"In fact, I do." A young man in a vicar's garb doffed his hat and walked forward. "You look in need of rest."

"Yes," she murmured, and couldn't help but let go the tears. "And so much more . . ."

The white border to his black cassock shone almost gold in the bright daylight. "We run a mission not far from here. Can you walk?"

"Barely," Nicole replied as she wiped below her eyes.

"It's not far. May I take your arm?"

The words of kindness caused more hot tears to trickle down her face. "I would be ever grateful."

He matched his longer strides to her halting steps while taking a great deal of her weight in his firm grip. "You will forgive me for saying so, madame, but you speak as one highborn."

"I am not married, sir." Nicole's words were so slurred she doubted whether he could understand her. "Nor could my beginnings have been any more humble."

"But you have suffered from the distresses of war?"

"Distresses," she repeated and would have wept had she still the strength. "Suffered."

They rounded a corner and faced a wood-slat church with a simple white steeple. Several newer buildings had been erected to the north—long, low establishments with open porches. The smaller of the two buildings was clearly a cookhouse because out of its tall chimney wafted an aroma so fine Nicole almost cried out from the pain awakened in her stomach.

"Not far now," the vicar said, helping her onward.

In the square formed by the church and its sister buildings a number of young children were playing. While poorly dressed, they appeared shiny clean and very happy. The vicar led her over to a long trestle table, eased her onto the bench, and motioned to one of the women standing near the cookhouse doorway. "A bowl of your soup and some bread, if you please, Mother."

"I'm afraid the soup's not quite done yet."

"I doubt very much," said the young vicar, "that our new guest will mind."

Nicole's hands trembled so she had difficulty holding the spoon, much less lifting it to her mouth. The first spoonful sloshed back into the bowl and onto the table. She looked up in dismay to find the woman from the cookhouse and the vicar both eyeing her with such compassion that Nicole found herself fighting back tears again.

"Just lift the bowl and sip, dearie," the woman said. "There's more than you who's come in here not able to manage them spoons."

She lowered her head so that all she needed to do was tip the bowl to her lips. She continued to shed tears as she drank the broth, all without understanding the reason why. Only after the last of the broth was down and she had used the spoon to scoop out the vegetables did she lift her gaze again. She didn't try to match the pair of smiles facing her, for to do so would release the floodgates of her weary heart. She merely whispered, "Forgive me."

"Ah, lass, there's not a thing on God's green earth you need to beg for less than forgiveness. Not from us, right, Father?"

"Perhaps the lady might care to tell us a bit of her story before you show her to a bed," the vicar said. "At the least her name."

"My name is Nicole Harrow."

For some reason, this caused both of them watching her to laugh out loud. "That's a fine name if ever I heard one," the woman declared. "Not a night goes by that I don't thank our Lord for another who shares your name. Charles Harrow, a saint I shall look for the instant I arrive in heaven."

"I have an uncle by that name." Her mind seemed gradually to disconnect itself from her body. It took all her effort to focus on the one task most important, which was to tear pieces from the bread. Her stomach was already becoming full, but still she managed to take in the bread in small bites. "And he is indeed a saint. I miss him terribly."

The two of them sat silent across the table from her. Nicole paid this no mind. Her entire self concentrated on the taste of the freshly baked bread, the feeling of good food settling into her stomach. Not to mention the feeling of being off her feet, seated now among smiling people. And the vicar had mentioned there would be a bed for her as well.

Clearing his throat, the vicar said, "You can't possibly be referring to the Lord Charles Harrow, Earl of Sutton?"

"Yes, that is my uncle Charles."

"And that would make you—"

Nicole gestured with the next to last piece of bread. "Yes, Lady Harrow. My uncle put the documents in my bag, and I didn't find them until we were at sea." She looked up at them, both now gaping at her openmouthed. "Whatever is the matter?" she asked.

"This . . . this is Harrow Hall," said the vicar.

Nicole would have laughed had she the energy. As it was, she could scarcely manage to say, "Impossible." She looked at the two before her. "Harrow Hall is in England."

The woman hurried into motion, scurrying around the table. "We'd best find this one a bed before she falls flat on her face." She lifted Nicole by the arm. "Come along, my dear. We'll have time for all these mysteries once you've rested and collected yourself."

Chapter 36

General Mitchell had experienced a truly dreadful day. Reports were coming in from all sides, so much of it conflicting information that he had no choice but to discount it all. One account had the British sending boatloads of spies ahead of a full-fledged invasion. Another suggested forays were preparing to extend right around the American garrison and move inland. He had reports that said the entire British garrison at New York was headed north, others claiming the regiments from Fort Ticonderoga were going down the Connecticut River to attack the colonials from Massachusetts all the way to Delaware. His French supply ships were weeks overdue, his men restless, and he was still awaiting orders from Philadelphia.

It was approaching midnight when he finally emerged from his office. The garrison headquarters was still a hive of activity, though most of the men bore the signs of bone weariness. Finding his adjutant likewise at his desk, the general barked, "Did I not order you away?"

"Yes, sir." The lieutenant pointed to a lone man seated by the front door. "This vicar has been waiting for almost six hours."

He vaguely recalled the man from when he attended a few Sunday services with the community. "Why haven't you seen to him?"

"He insists that he has information for your ears alone."

"Not another," the general groaned, then stumped over and stood in front of the man, towering over him. "Forgive me, Father, but this is not the best of days for a visit."

"I understand, sir." The vicar was the senior cleric of Cambridge and showed the hardship of war across his broad features. "I would not have dreamed of bothering you, except for something my younger associate came upon today. Something I have decided requires your urgent attention."

"Yes, all right, what is it then?"

"He found a young woman wandering the streets today and so brought her back to the hostel. She was much the worse for wear, I can tell you. So much so, I scarcely wished to question her at all. But she knew things, General. Things which left me speechless. She claims, well . . ." The vicar fingered his watch chain uncertainly.

"Speak up, Father! You can't begin to believe the fables I've already been told this day."

"Precisely, sir. That is what I thought as well. Mere fables. Only this lady, she says she's a friend of Pastor Collins, who runs our Boston seminary. And when I inquired further of her, she knew things that led me to believe she spoke the truth."

General Mitchell stifled a yawn. A hot meal and his bed were what he needed at the moment. "So she knows this pastor on the wrong side of the Charles River."

"No, sir. Well, yes, that is true. But it is what *else* she claims to know that has brought me here to you."

By now the adjutant and men from several other offices were moving in closer toward General Mitchell and the vicar.

"Such as?" the general asked.

"Sir, she claims to have dined the night before last with the British commandant and all the officer corps of the British army!"

The general and his men found this a reason for late-night mirth. "Please forgive us," he said. "It has been a long day. The high command dined with her, did you say?"

"And their wives too. In honor of the prince regent's birthday."

That stilled all laughter. The general glanced at his number two man. They had only learned of the gathering earlier that very afternoon. "You don't say."

"I do indeed, General. I probed as deeply as I dared, sir. She described things about the commandant's private quarters that, well, they baffled me. Plain and simple. Utterly baffled me."

The general was now hemmed in on all sides by his men. "What else did she tell you?"

"That the British are in disagreement among themselves. She heard two specific arguments as to what they should do with the troops marching down from . . . wait, I wrote the name out so as not to mistake it" From his cassock the vicar pulled out a scrap of paper. "Ticonderoga. Did I say that correctly?"

The general spun about and ordered, "Have my horse saddled at once."

"The lady says this information is given as a sign that she is who she claims, which is another amazement, I don't mind telling you. She also says that men with even more important information are being held in the Cambridge stockade as spies. And that you have another man among your company, someone close to you, who is actually spying for the British."

The general saw his men exchange astonished looks. They too had heard rumors of a spy operating around headquarters. "What did you say was this lady's name?"

"I did not say, sir. Purposely I did not, to avoid being laughed from headquarters." The vicar fumbled nervously with the cross hanging from his neck. "She . . . she claims to be the Viscountess Lady Nicole Harrow."

The general's roar caused the chandelier to shiver. "Where on earth is my horse?"

Chapter 37

The night turned out to be an interminable wait. Gordon's earlier calm had given way to as great a temptation as he had ever faced, to worry and seek to vent his anger at being imprisoned again. But this time he found himself in a quiet corner, one where he could sit and reflect on all that had happened. He was weary, yes. But it wasn't just a question of getting enough sleep. That afternoon he had dozed and woken and yet felt the same as before he slept. He wasn't a man given to reflecting that much. Gordon had always lived for action. But there was something he sensed about himself now, an inner compass working that he could describe only as some connection to God. He felt himself being drawn inward.

With the stars for companions and the music of hissing torches and crackling campfires around him, he looked at himself. He permitted the questions to surface, those questions no man could answer and from which all strong men sought to flee. Where was he headed? What was he to do with his life? Was there a reason for his strength and his gift of leading others beyond that of satisfying his own ambitions? What of all that had brought him to this point, the hard experience of being a young man at sea, alone and bullied by those bigger, his gradual rise up the ranks, his command of as fine a vessel as ever floated, only to have it stolen out from under him? Had all this been gradually bringing him to this point, so that he might sit imprisoned within a foul military stockade and ask himself these questions? If so, what was the purpose for tomorrow? The only basis for meaning in this tide of wonder seemed that he was to *do* something. *Accomplish* something. *Achieve* that which, without these experiences and realizations and questions, would remain beyond him.

Yet he had no idea what that new purpose might be. He didn't feel any more aware of the road ahead than he had before. In fact, he felt even less sure than before. The strangest component of this entire night was how much at peace he felt in spite of all the floundering.

There could only be one answer, he decided. One course that made any sense at all. And although it galled him mightily to admit it, he knew he must continue to wait. He must pray and seek what the Lord would have him do.

Close to dawn Gordon felt the chill enclosing him as tightly as the prison walls. However, this too seemed unable to penetrate the cloak of peace, the armor of strength that was most certainly not his own. Even here he could sense the Lord's hand. He wondered how often before he had ignored what he was convinced now could only be a gift from above.

The stars remained bright, then came the first hint of dawn. A hue and cry alerted the guards walking the parapet to a change in the making. There was a clatter of many horses and the angry shouts of an officer being made to wait.

While Gordon couldn't make out the words, he somehow knew. He crossed to where his men slept huddled together on a bedding of straw and filthy blankets. John Jackson and the bosun were the first to notice him, and they nudged the others awake. A good man, Gordon decided, this honorable soldier, despite his scoundrel-like appearance. Nicole had most definitely chosen well.

Gordon crouched down and whispered, "I think it is time. We'd best make ourselves ready for inspection."

Together they went over to the horses' drinking trough and one by one washed their hands, faces, and necks. Gordon watched as they tried to clean their ratty clothing of straw and mud, then tied their hair back in the fashion of jolly Jack-tars. Fine men, he reflected, the thought full of gratitude for their company. Too much to keep inside, he murmured, "I owe each and every one of you a debt I can never repay."

The men were no doubt unaccustomed to such words, especially the tone of quiet affection Gordon had used. As one they left it to the bosun to reply, "We're just going about our duty, sir."

"No, you are not. I don't know what lies ahead, but whatever it is, I would count it a blessing if I could remain in your company." He repeated, "A blessing," the power of its meaning resounding within him.

Behind him the stockade doors creaked open. Carter stiffened and said, "It's the same ones as arrested us, Skipper."

"Go and gather your belongings," said Gordon.

As Gordon started to turn away, John Jackson halted him. "I'm understanding what it is Miss Nicole has found in you, sir."

Gordon offered the man his hand. "I would hope to count you among us."

"Ho there, you prisoner!" The chief jailer stomped across the yard while buttoning his vest. "The officer wants a word right away. Step smartly!"

Gordon strode over to the waiting officer and offered a salute. "Good morning, sir."

The officer held to none of his humor of the previous day. "It appears I owe you an apology, Captain."

"Accepted," Gordon said.

But the officer didn't seem to be finished. His mustache twitched under the strain of forming the words. "I have heard from the general himself how critical it is that I ensure there are no hard feelings and that—"

"You did your duty, sir."

"So I thought at the time," the officer said stiffly.

"So I would have done as well," said Gordon. "Which is precisely what I will tell the general if he asks." He ended the discussion by pointing to the horses brought over by the officer's men. "Are those mounts for us?"

"They are."

"Then let's be off."

But when Gordon and his men were all mounted, the officer held his ground. He looked Gordon straight in the eye and saluted smartly. "Your servant, sir."

Gordon returned the salute and then extended his hand. "Gordon Goodwind, formerly of His Majesty's merchant navy."

"Lawrence Harries, Major, New York Mounted Rifles." The man's grip was firm as iron, a sign of one long used to the rigors of cavalry. "The general's compliments. He finds himself in a serious quandary."

"A request, Major. I would prefer to carry on this conversation beyond these prison gates."

"Most certainly."

But as Gordon urged his horse about, the chief jailer suddenly appeared. "Just a minute here! Where do you think you're going with this lot?"

"They are yours no longer." Major Harries produced a paper from his greatcoat pocket. "General Mitchell has personally requested their company."

Gordon left the jailer standing there studying the document as he raised his hand and called, "Forward, men!"

The major proved a decent sort by not speaking again until they'd put a goodly stretch of road and forest behind them. He finally said, "Your pardon, Captain."

"Not a captain anymore," Gordon corrected, then wondered at how he could make this admission without feeling a stab of pain. Fifteen years of his life he had given to gaining that post. Fifteen years. "Gordon will do quite well."

"I have no doubt the general will have something to say about this," the major predicted. "Be that as it may, the general finds himself, shall we say, at odds with a certain lady."

"Then," Gordon replied wryly, "I pity the general."

"I would have to agree. And General Mitchell has learned from the lady that there is a spy among us."

Gordon felt the icy knot in his gut. "That is true," he said.

The major obviously noted the change in his tone and called out, "Rider!" Immediately one of his men broke ranks and cantered forward. The major carefully continued, "The lady also said that once you were free, you would give us the spy's name."

Gordon couldn't hide his smile, and he heard several of his men chuckle. The major asked him, "Have I said something humorous?"

"We are all admiring the lady's talent," Gordon answered. "She has saved us yet again."

"And the name of our infiltrator, sir?"

Gordon lost his smile. "Henri Robichaud," he said.

"Spell that, please." Major Harries used his pommel to steady the parchment on which he penciled the name. He then crammed the paper into the rider's hand and ordered, "Take this straight to the general. Ride!"

Chapter 38

Nicole spotted Gordon just as he returned the guard officer's salute and guided his horse into the headquarters' courtyard. Instantly she left the side porch where they were seated and flew through the general's office and out the front door and down the stairs. Gordon slid from his horse to greet her. The dress she wore was too large, and she tripped on the bottom step. She would have sprawled in the dust had he not been there to catch her fall.

"I say," the major drawled, "I wouldn't mind having such a salute upon my own arrival at headquarters."

The general stepped through the portico. "That might be a trifle difficult to arrange, Major. But I shall see what I can do."

Major Harries sprang to attention and saluted his superior officer. "Mission accomplished, sir."

"So I see. And all misunderstandings corrected, I hope," he said, wiping his hands on his breakfast napkin.

"Aye, sir. The apology was accepted by the captain."

"None was required," interjected Gordon from the bottom step, "not from an officer doing his duty in wartime." Gordon couldn't very well salute the general, as Nicole was holding his arm. So he made do with a bow instead. "Your servant, sir."

"Perhaps you will be willing to accept my apology as well."

"Not necessary, as I have said."

"Ah, but it was my word that put you on the list of enemies." Then the general's expression turned sour, and he asked his adjutant, "Any word on that Robichaud fellow?"

"Not yet, sir." The young officer's tone sounded distressed. "But squads are scouring the region this very minute."

"Well, bring Robichaud here as soon as you locate him." The general waved Gordon and Nicole inside. "Perhaps you might care for a bite of breakfast."

Gordon replied, "I'd prefer to see to my men first, General."

The general's gaze sharpened. "Major Harries will see to it they're all fed, bathed and clothed from the slop chest." He squinted at the man on the horse behind Gordon and asked, "Is that one of our men I see there?"

"Aye, sir," Jackson said, dismounting. "Sergeant John Jackson."

"Well met, Sergeant. It appears I also owe you an apology. Would you care to join us?"

Gordon objected, "We are in need of some cleaning up, sir."

"We've all eaten more road dust than is good for us, Captain." The general returned through the front door, calling as he walked, "Three more places for breakfast!"

Gordon turned to Nicole and whispered, "That is a most interesting frock."

"It was the smallest they had on hand at Harrow Hall."

"Where?"

"Never mind. I'll explain later." She looked around at the company of men watching them and grinning. "You are well?" she said, still holding his arm.

"At this very moment, seeing you and the dawn

together and as a free man, I am as close to health and happiness as a mortal might ever hope to come."

"If you'll pardon me," Major Harries said, tipping his hat to Nicole. "Ma'am, I can't begin to say how much I regret my words earlier."

Her smile and nod said more than words.

Carter cleared his throat and said, "On behalf of all the men, my lady, we'd like to offer you our thanks. For everything."

"It is none less than what you would have done for me," Nicole replied, addressing them all. "And have done numerous times in the past."

The men offered her and Gordon both salutes and farewells as they departed. With John Jackson on one side and Gordon on the other, Nicole walked through the crowded main hall and entered the side veranda. The general waved them over and said, "Please, sit down and take your fill."

As Gordon and Jackson shifted their attention to the welcoming repast, the general continued, "Miss Nicole has refused to discuss the matter until you gentlemen arrived. But now, with your permission, the matters of war can wait no longer."

"Most certainly, sir." Gordon said, holding back from saluting the general with a biscuit in his hand.

"My initial inquiries have proven futile. I have yet to find anyone who has ridden with this Henri Robichaud. The man has a reputation as a fighter and a loner with a fierce temper. He is shunned by one and all."

"I am not the least surprised," said Nicole. She pushed aside her plate. The excellent meal now sat like a stone in her stomach.

"Why do you say that, ma'am?"

"For one thing, the name itself is a falsehood."

The general and his retinue all fastened their eyes on her. "I beg your pardon?" the general said.

"It is not this man's real name," she confirmed. "The real Henri Robichaud is my father."

She watched consternation grow among the gathered men, and she sensed more officers crowding in from behind. The general required a moment to collect himself. "Forgive me, but you have said your name is Harrow."

"That is correct," Nicole said. Her regret now became a physical pain. The collection of strangers viewing her and hearing every word couldn't stop her from looking to Gordon and saying, "You cannot imagine the sorrow it causes me to have you hear certain new portions of my history in such a manner."

Gordon took her hand in his and said, "Before all men and before God, I tell you I will always be grateful to have met you and to have come to care for you as I do."

"I say," the general murmured.

"Tell them what you must," Gordon quietly urged her.

Nicole took a breath. "I was born the daughter of Andrew and Catherine Harrow, in the province now known as Nova Scotia. My mother's closest friend was a Frenchwoman from the neighboring Acadian village. She had a daughter, Anne, who was both very weak and constantly ill. There was no French doctor available, and the British doctors refused to treat a French baby. So the mothers traded babies so that Catherine could take Anne to Halifax. While they were away, the British concluded a series of raids. Every Frenchman, woman, and child was expelled from their homeland."

"Forgive me," the general interrupted. "How old were you?"

"Twelve weeks." She held her gaze on Gordon, who knew this much and strengthened her resolve with the care in his eyes. "The ships took my people to every corner of the earth. Families were separated, never to be reunited. We were at least fortunate enough to remain together, and alive. Of the seven ships bound for Charleston, only ours and one other ever made it. We spent almost eight years living from hand to mouth, begging work wherever we could. Finally we heard that the Spanish were offering land and seeds and tools to any Acadians willing to go and settle the bayou territory of the Louisiana province. The trek south took us over a year, for we had to stop often and labor for food and supplies."

She glanced at the general and saw a man who looked like he had been struck a blow. "My father, Henri Robichaud, is one of the finest men who has ever walked the earth. It is only because of his strength, and the strength of his faith, that I am alive today. I, my family, my village, and many other villages besides. He is more than mayor of our town. He is a leader who should be wearing a crown. Henri would never be party to such a cruel betrayal. I feel ashamed that I even doubted this."

It took the general a long moment to find his voice. "Then who is the imposter?"

"We must wait till the man arrives to find that out," she said.

"But you suspect someone?"

"From the description Gordon gave me," Nicole said slowly, "I fear so."

A hail from the front sentry drew them all around. Several of the officers rushed out, and one returned to announce, "It appears the Frenchie is here, sir."

The general was already up. He tossed his napkin on his plate and offered Nicole his hand. "If you please, my lady."

She was unable to answer nor give adequate strength to her legs. Although she wanted all this behind her, still it was terrifying to rise and face what she thought might lie ahead.

The general remained still a moment, a compact and battered warrior whose outstretched hand had been molded by years of reins and saber and command. "While

257

I battle against everything that British nobility symbolizes, just now I can think of no other title for you than 'my lady.' " He gave a military bow. "My lady, if you will accompany me, please."

The squad filling the headquarters' courtyard was spread out in the casual manner of men who had spent far too long in the saddle. The horses and riders were coated liberally with dust and muck. Three men stood well back from the others, stationed to block the only way in or out. The man at their center was neither a prisoner nor free. He sat easy and low atop his steed, the leather slouch hat concealing the upper two-thirds of his face. But what Nicole could see clearly—the indolent mouth, the handsome chin, the broad shoulders, the long raven black hair—was enough to freeze her soul.

"Steady there, my lady," the general said, his grip now firm on her arm. "Remember, you are among friends here."

The general's words were muffled by Nicole's rising fury. This man had not only lied about his identity, he had stolen her father's good name and taken money in return for the casual destruction of her beloved. Nicole's body shook with rage.

The squad leader saluted General Mitchell. "Lieutenant Rightly, sir. I've brought him straight here as ordered."

"Well done, Lieutenant. You and your men remain as you are." The general then raised his voice and barked, "You there, whoever you are, remove your hat!"

With an arrogant sweep, the rider flipped his hat back so it hung from his neck by a leather braid. The dark gaze slid across Nicole's face. He drawled in French, "Still wearing castoffs and hand-me-downs, I see."

"Enough!" The general's face had gone brilliant red. "Do you know this man, my lady?"

"*My lady*," mocked the man, his English heavily accented. "My lady, indeed! She is nothing more than an ignorant village lass, who will sing any tune you wish so long as it earns her a meal and a bed!"

"Hold hard there!" Gordon stepped to the forefront, his eyes blazing.

The Frenchman rocked back in his saddle. "You!"

"That is right, traitor, it's Gordon Goodwind. And if you have a mind to see tomorrow, you will address the lady as such!"

The Frenchman made an obvious attempt to recover. "General, you cannot possibly accept the word of a spy and a trollop against my—"

"Enough of that!" General Mitchell rapped out again. "My lady, do you recognize this man?"

"Yes I do, sir."

"His name, if you please."

Nicole swallowed, her eyes steady on the man. "His name is Jean Dupree."

Chapter 39

Major Harries offered a gloved hand and said, "I will be happy to hold the reins, Miss Nicole."

"Thank you, sir." She waited for Gordon to dismount and come around. She needed no assistance, but it felt good to draw from his strength at this time. "It is most kind of you to see us out here."

"General's orders, ma'am. And my pleasure." The major lifted his voice and called up to the stockade's parapet, "Ho there! Official visitors from General Mitchell to see the prisoner Jean Dupree!"

Soon the tall prison gates swung open, and she and Gordon started forward. Gordon commented shortly, "Never did I think I would willingly pass through these portals again."

The stench of overcrowded men wafted out. "I could never do this without you," she said weakly. "Never."

"You need not do this at all."

"Yes," she replied, walking through the gates and nodding to the waiting chief jailer. "I must."

"Very well, then." Gordon addressed the startled jailer, "Gordon Goodwind and the Lady Nicole Harrow to see Jean Dupree."

"He's back in the cage with the others doomed as traitors." The jailer gave Gordon a wary look, but when

Gordon said nothing, he merely pointed them toward the guard hut. "I'll ask you to wait in there while I bring the prisoner out."

The wait seemed to last forever, though it couldn't have been more than a few minutes before Jean Dupree towered in the doorway. "Come to gloat over me?" he demanded.

Nicole debated whether she should order him to speak in English, then decided it didn't matter. She could translate for Gordon later. "I have come to say that I have begged the general for your release," she said in French, "and Gordon has aided me in this." She motioned him to the seat across from them. "Sit down, please."

Reluctantly Jean lowered himself down, while three armed guards stood careful watch nearby. His chains clinked when he leaned forward and rested his arms on the table. His next words were in English and directed at Gordon. "You know what she has just told me?"

"I don't know much French, but from your expression I imagine she has said how she has asked the general for your pardon. And I have added what weight I could to the request. But he's having none of it, I'm sorry to say."

A hint of Nicole's former ire remained with her still. The taste of ashes was bitter in her mouth, not only from the anger she had felt before, but also because of the love she'd wasted on this man. All night she had prayed, and once again God had seemed silent. Yet this time the stillness had been answer enough. For through this nighttime vigil had come a sense of rightness. She carried it with her even here. "We will do all we can to have your sentence lessened. For the moment, they are remaining very severe."

"Then there is little hope of success," Jean Dupree responded with a smirk. He seemed altogether unfazed by what she'd just said. "Seeing as how I am to hang in four days' time."

Nicole studied the man who had first stolen her heart, then robbed her nights, her mind, of peace. "What brought you to such a grievous betrayal?"

"Your father had me banished." Although his speech held to a casual tone, there was fire in his eyes. "In revenge I took his name and besmirched it everywhere I possibly could."

"Besides his faith, his good name is what my father prizes most," she reproached him.

"Well do I know it." The smile was tainted with bitterness, anger. "I cannot tell you what pleasure I have had in building him a new reputation that stretches now from Louisiana to Boston."

She nodded slowly, praying inwardly that Henri would never learn of this. But all she said was, "I forgive you. And if it comes to it, I know Father will also."

The calm way she expressed this left Jean clearly stunned.

"The real reason why I came to you this day," she replied, "why both of us are here, is to share with you the message of God's love for you."

Gordon said, "We, who have every reason to hate you, come now with a message of peace. As one who was placed in the hangman's cage by your very hand, I urge you to think on where you are headed."

Beneath the table Nicole reached over and gripped Gordon's hand. It felt as though her heart were about to burst, but she forced herself to stay composed. "See this as a moment when you can still choose your final destiny," she said. "Choose wisely, while you still have the time."

Chapter 40

Nicole reached up to push back a tendril of hair that had tumbled across her forehead. Her Bible lay open in her lap, but her eyes were closed. She'd read the Scripture passage often enough over the past days to know it by heart. It spoke to her in a new way each time she recited it to herself. It was Gordon who had drawn her attention to these verses in the Gospel of Matthew. She smiled at the thought. Strange that she had felt she must lead him into spiritual truths, and now it was he who was leading her.

She had been familiar with the passage. Both sets of parents had at various times tried to instill the words within her, yet for some reason they had only touched her mind, not her heart. Perhaps she hadn't needed them in such an intense way before. She needed them now. Had perhaps always needed them but had refused to recognize the fact. She opened her eyes and stared into the distance where a lone driver prodded a team of oxen pulling a cart weighed down with newly mown hay. Nicole could smell the freshness of it even from where she sat on the vine-covered veranda, sheltered from the burn of the afternoon sun.

The words were spoken by Christ himself.

"Ye have heard that it hath been said, Thou shalt love thy neighbour, and hate thine enemy.

"But I say unto you, Love your enemies, bless them that curse you, do good to them that hate you, and pray for them which despitefully use you, and persecute you;

"That ye may be the children of your Father which is in heaven."

In spite of the heaviness of her heart as she thought of the conflict in the world she knew, she smiled to herself. She felt she was finally beginning to grasp the deeper meaning of the verses before her. What a different place the world would be if people lived by the words of the blessed Book.

She sighed. Her world was again headed for war. Was already in deep conflict. There was no peace. No peace.

"Ah." The one small sound escaped her lips. She laid her head against the high-backed rocker, again closing her eyes against the intensity of her feelings. There could be peace. There was peace. Wonderful, glorious peace within individual hearts. With God's help and forgiveness she had discovered it for herself, once she had let go of the bitterness and pain of her past. For the first time she felt she truly understood the two sets of parents who had given and sustained her life. They knew the passage. Not just the words but the truth in the words. The God of the words. This was why they had not fallen into bitterness. What was it Pastor Collins had said about the response of different soils to the same rains? Some soil became soft and pliable, other soil hard-packed and resistant. Why had it taken her so long to see this?

Again Nicole thought of the words of the passage. The truth had been there, right before her all the time. God forgives when forgiveness is given. There can be no joy or comfort in an embittered heart. For the follower of the Christ, there was no other choice but forgiveness.

Her smile deepened. She couldn't describe the relief

to her soul to have this peace within, the bitterness now gone through which she had once viewed her world. At first she had felt almost a void. The anger had become such a part of her, to have it taken away had left a vacancy. Yet this was soon filled up as she turned to the pages of Scripture. The change had been beyond her dreams and expectation. Every day she felt the inner quickening. The sky appeared brighter, the birdsongs sounded sweeter. She felt more alive than ever. Even in the midst of the deepest of traumas her inner peace brought her a settledness, stability now. It was a *miracle*. There was that word again.

The prayer that rose from her heart was one of deep-felt gratitude to a God who understood her far better than she understood herself.

Gordon called on her that evening, a regular occurrence now among the events of the day. Each time she heard his approaching footsteps, her heart felt a tremor of anticipation.

Their greeting was warm but discreet. Within the small Cambridge inn where Nicole resided, curious eyes seemed to be everywhere.

"It has been unseasonably warm today," Gordon observed as he placed his hat in Nicole's outstretched hand.

"It is much cooler on the back porch," she said. "Do you wish for shade?"

"I have no desire to discredit your name—" he began, but Nicole quickly put his uncertainties to rest.

"Two of the household servants are working in the back garden," she explained.

Gordon nodded, relief in his eyes. "Some mercy from the sun's blast does sound good."

"I have drawn some fresh water from the well."

She watched a moment as Gordon retreated to the porch, heavily screened by ivy, and lowered himself into one of the hickory twig chairs and stretched out his legs. She hurried toward the well.

"It is much cooler here, is it not?" Nicole asked as she poured out two cups of the cold water and set the pitcher on a small wicker table. She handed the cup to Gordon, and their fingers brushed slightly. Nicole dropped her eyes and felt her cheeks warm.

"It is," Gordon said. "Very much so. I've never felt such heat, even when out drilling troops in the midday sun. But we did much of our training in the forested valley down below the fort. Sergeant Jackson is proving to be worth his weight in gold, I don't mind telling you. We might easily have lost half the men to heatstroke, had John not suggested we train among the trees."

Nicole's heart sank at the mention of preparing for battles to come. He must have seen it, for he hurried on, "What has busied your day?"

"Very little. I feel rather useless living such as I do. I did a bit of mending of tunics. And I did go in to market with my basket. There wasn't much to be found. It is a blessing we have the gardens and the hens."

She lifted her cup and moved to the chair near Gordon. Both remained silent with their thoughts. At length Gordon broke the silence.

"I came this evening with a heaviness of spirit," he said slowly, "with a very small but intense hope that will not die."

Nicole lifted her head and looked into his face.

"You know that I have sought before to share my heart with you. You stopped me then and wisely so. It was not the proper time to speak, just as you said," he said, his words coming faster now.

Nicole could feel her heart thumping within her

chest. She prayed she would remain calm, think clearly.

"What to me was once a mystery—that a maid would turn away the suit of an honorable man simply because he did not hold to faith in the same way she herself did—I now see as justified. I admire you for placing the choice before me. Had I known then the difference between believing that there is a God and believing that I must of necessity throw myself on His mercy, I would have understood your position without question. I must thank you for your stability of faith."

High compliments, all. But not the words Nicole most desired to hear.

Gordon cleared his throat, switched the position of his booted feet, and continued, "I fear that we have put ourselves in a very delicate position. I am unsure as to what your situation might be in regard to returning to Nova Scotia, but I expect that British shores will no longer bid you welcome. As for me, I know I dare not ever present myself to my homeland again. There is no turning back, Nicole. I have given my allegiance to this new land of America. I intend to also give my heart in loyalty. Win or lose the battle that is surely before us, I am now on the side of the colonists, whatever the cost. This will be my home."

He paused and she nodded silently. "What you say is true," she said, her voice sounding surprisingly low and steady to her own ears. "There is no turning back. We have cast our lot."

"That does not trouble you?"

"It troubles me greatly. Good men will die in this war, and wives will lose their husbands. Mothers will lose sons, children their fathers. It makes no sense to me. But we cannot choose the world in which we live. The conflict is already here. We are here. And we have chosen the side we must be on. What can one do but pray and trust our very lives to God? If I never see my parents again—" she paused a moment to collect herself. "Well, I cannot, nor would I ever choose to hide my grief. I will grieve if our country continues to be torn by war. But sailing back to England is not an option for me. This is my country."

Then an unexpected boldness took hold of Nicole. She raised her head and looked directly into the eyes of the man before her. "And I should grieve even more should this war rend from me one whom I have come to love with all my heart."

"Do you mean there is hope, and this anguish of heart may yet be stilled?" His voice was barely heard, yet the words were clear.

Tears gathered in her eyes. "There need be no anguish," she answered, "so long as there is love."

He reached to take her hand in both of his. "There is love, my darling Nicole. Unspeakable love. I have agonized over my desire to tell you so, but I did not know if I dared to hope, unworthy as I am. I have nothing—absolutely nothing to offer a viscountess."

She pressed his hands to her face, and he could feel the dampness of her tears. "Do not speak of unworthiness," she said. "Before God we are both unworthy, yet He saw fit to freely give us His grace. And do not speak of the viscountess. She has served her purpose and is no longer needed. Here we are all equal and beginning anew." Her smile came from her heart, and she kissed his hand. "And, Gordon," she continued, "you do have everything to offer. Where there is love, there is everything we truly need."

Gordon lifted her hand and kissed it in return.

Their eyes met, as though for the first time, as though for all eternity. In that moment, all worries over the past and anxieties over the future were stilled. Here was the shelter of each other. Here, at last, was love.

Authors' Note

Early that summer, the new British commandant of His Majesty King George III's Royal Colonial Army ordered a secret evacuation of all Loyalist forces from Boston. Under the cover of night, the entire garrison was removed.

By early July, Boston and its surroundings were firmly in the hands of the American forces, commanded by General George Washington.

The British never returned.

————— ❧ —————

Watch for *The Beloved Land*
in the fall of 2002.